# FEARLESS

——————————————

ELITE DOMS OF WASHINGTON

## ELIZABETH SAFLEUR

Elizabeth SaFleur LLC
PO Box 6395
Charlottesville, VA 22906
Elizabeth@ElizabethSaFleur.com
www.ElizabethSaFleur.com

Edited by Patricia A. Knight
Cover Design: Cosmic Letterz

**ISBN:** 978-1-949076-09-7

*Dear Reader:*
*This book is a work of fiction, not reality. My characters operate in a compressed time frame. A real-world scenario involves getting to know one another more extensively than my characters do before engaging in BDSM activities. Please learn as much as you can before trying any activity you read about in erotic fiction. Talk to people in your local BDSM group. Nearly every community has one. Get to know people slowly, and always be careful. Share your hopes, dreams and fears with anyone before playing with them, have a safeword and share it with your Dom or Domme (they can't read your mind), use protection, and have a safe-call or other backup in place. Remember: Safe, Sane and Consensual. Or, no play. May you find that special person to honor and love you the way you wish. You deserve that.*
*~XO, Elizabeth*

# PRELUDE

"Washington, DC." Steffan nodded. "I need to make the fundraising rounds. It's time to get my nonprofit the attention it deserves."

"But in the States?"

"Yes, and I'd like you with me. You can finally get that degree. I hear George Washington University has the best physical therapy program. What do you say?"

Laurent scratched his five o'clock shadow. "You want out of Stockholm."

The man didn't respond, which told Laurent he was right.

"Don't you think it's time we do something different?" Steffan asked.

"I'm not as self-destructive as I was in Amsterdam." Laurent began to pace. "But I know you don't want to leave me to my own devices. I thank you for rescuing me, and I would be content to be wherever you were, if I, alone, made you happy. I love you like a brother, but you and I both know you may not be enough for me, and I can't be what you need sexually or as a submissive—not fully. How's this going to work? I will do anything for you, Steffan, but I cannot change my gender." He lifted his eyes to the person closest to him in the world—in all ways except physically.

"Which is why we should go to DC. There's a way for both of us to have what we need."

"Oh?"

"Do you remember that Domme I scened with at Club 501? In London?"

"She was rather unforgettable."

"She's a founding member of a private, secret club called Accendos. I want both of us to join."

Laurent examined his best friend for a few moments. "When can we leave?"

# 1

The soft-close doors on her fire-engine red Maserati Gran-Turismo made a soft thunk. The elegant machine gave a quiet chirp when she hit the key fob.

With a grimace, Sarah shifted on her new Valentino Rockstud patent-leather pumps and limped to the garage elevator for Club Accendos.

While the heels were to-die-for gorgeous, an hour ago she'd lost all feeling but pain in her feet. She'd been on them since eight that morning with three client dress fittings, including one Senator's wife who could not make up her mind—as if choosing a blue tulle A-line over a black crepe shift was akin to national security. Ah, well, beauty had its price, and in the end, all that mattered was that her patrons were happy.

With any luck, she'd make it to her private bedroom unnoticed despite what had to be a large crowd in the club. The garage was full. Thank god for her reserved parking space. She needed a lavender-scented bath and eight hours of blissful, uninterrupted sleep.

The elevator doors slid open, and she came face to face with the owner of Club Accendos, Alexander Rockingham.

"Sarah, just who I was looking for." He stepped back to allow her to pass.

"Hello, Alexander, aren't you on your way out?" Ignoring the complaint from her throbbing feet, she rose on tip-toes and gave him a peck on the cheek.

"I saw you come in on the security camera. Have a minute for a walk in the garden? Everything's in bloom, and it won't take long." He jutted out his elbow in invitation.

"Of course." She slipped her arm through his. For her friend of fifteen years, she had all the minutes in the world to give. To hell with her aching feet.

"By the way, nice car. What made you decide on a Maserati?"

"It's beautiful? It purrs?" she offered with an unapologetic laugh. "Indulgent, I know. What can I say? I have a weakness for pretty things. Besides, if I have to be stuck in DC traffic as often as I am, I might as well do it in style."

"Nothing more than you deserve. You're working too hard, aren't you?" Alexander's handsome face formed a concerned frown.

She shrugged lightly and patted the arm that held hers. "It's spring. It's what I do, though I thought Mrs. Darden would never make up her mind this morning. When she finally did, she chose the first of the fifteen dresses she tried on."

"That brings me to good news. Your charity fashion show last week broke a new record. The battered women's shelter will be able to add 300 beds with the $200,000 raised."

"*We* raised," she reminded him. "I'm thrilled. I can't thank you enough for getting Senator Markson there. Perhaps I can get her to come to my next one. I've decided four events a year isn't enough. We should do more."

4

"Ambitious."

"It's the least I can do. I spend my days fitting the wealthy and elite of D.C. in Gucci and Prada, while the Washington Shelter for Women and Children does meaningful work. They give people their lives back." While as a personal stylist and wardrobe consultant, she had the ability to enjoy luxury and glamour, she would never lose touch with what was really important in this world—freedom to live your life without fear. "So, was that what you wanted to talk to me about?"

"No, I have a request. Let's talk where it's more … private." As they strolled leisurely down the hallway, he nodded at the security team standing before the massive oak doors leading into the Club's main play space, The Library.

An arousing series of slaps followed by a man's long wail filtered through the closed doors. She grinned. "My, we're starting early today."

Alexander chuckled. "You know what they say about spring. It brings all the boys and girls out to play."

She made a small murmur of agreement as they strode by. How easily she could dart upstairs to her private room and slip into a dress, perhaps the red one with the lacing up the back which coupled nicely with her new Chanel black suede boots. Having a man crawl to her, lower the zipper with his teeth … *mmmm. Perhaps another time.* She'd made other plans for her rare weekend off. Plans were important. Having the discipline to stick to them was more important, and one of her rules was only Alexander could interrupt them.

They entered the long breezeway, blessedly empty, that led to the back of the house. Her breath stilled at the view through the glass French doors that opened to the stone terrace. Alexander's extensive, walled grounds were a sight to behold in any season, but as if overnight, every flowering tree, shrub, and flower bed, had burst into a color—whites, reds, blues, violets, yellows, and oranges, against a backdrop of every shade of green. The color warmed her soul. She'd outfitted too many people today in drab navy blue and black.

"Washington DC springs are spectacular, aren't they?" Alexander cracked open the doors, and the scents of rich earth and roses drifted over her.

"Nothing like them. So what's this other news? Clearly it must be bad if you're trying to distract me with your enchanted gardens."

He winked at her. "Plan foiled. We have two new candidates for membership."

"Ah, I see. No one else can do it? I had hoped to take off a few days." She often vetted new members for Alexander and determined if they were a good fit for their Accendos family before they presented the application to the seven members of the club's Tribunal Council. This weekend, however? She needed some much-delayed "me" time—and sleep. Insomnia couldn't last forever, though this recent bout was testing that limit.

"I'm sure they can, but a request has been made for you, specifically. Let's walk."

"Oh? Don't tell me. A famous politician? Military general?"

"Not exactly."

Now she was intrigued. It never ceased to amaze her that Alexander had kept Club Accendos secret for so long. Ninety-nine percent of the town had no clue his mansion on Q street in Georgetown was the private play space of the kinky elite—members of the U.S. Congress, military heads, and other bastions of Washington DC power.

They stepped down the three wide steps to pause at the Greek God of erotic yearning. Pothos looked down upon them from his center stage placement in the oval. As she often did, she sent up a silent prayer of thanks to him for whatever force was responsible for connecting her to Alexander, the man she called mentor, brother and sometimes, in her heart, father. An overwhelming sense of gratitude for her well-ordered and privileged life arose—as it often did when she stood in his gardens.

She eased off her heels, hooking them over her index finger. Normally she'd never take them off, as they were important to her overall presentation, but, as usual, Accendos' permissive atmosphere urged her to take a moment of pleasure. The sunlight had warmed the stones, and her toes stretched in delicious freedom.

"You said these potential members asked for me?" With eyes closed, she lifted her face and let the sunshine pour over her. *Heaven.*

"Yes, Derek met them in Copenhagen. Apparently one of them was quite complimentary of you. That's why Derek felt he could invite Steffan to check us out."

Her eyes snapped open. "Excuse me, did you say Steffan?"

"Steffan Vidar. He impressed Derek. Watched him handle three female submissives at once, and now that he's moving to DC—"

"Wait. He's moving to DC? To here?"

"You know this man?"

*Know him.* Familiar regret followed by a budding panic swelled up inside. "I met him in London. Club 501. It was a while ago." She lifted her foot and put a heel back on, then the other.

"I sense you don't agree with Derek's assessment of him?"

"Oh, no, it's not that ..." She stepped around the fountain. How could she talk to Alexander about Steffan? He couldn't be moving to DC. He said he'd never leave Sweden, never leave "those who depended on him." His exact words that morning she'd left him—after a night that *never* should have happened.

"Do I need to know something about this gentleman, Sarah? He seemed rather eager to see you. A little too eager in my estimation. He was quite … adamant."

"You talked to him." She stopped in front of him, having made a full circle of Pothos.

"Of course. No one steps foot in this place without speaking with me." He smiled as if trying to put her at ease. "Derek seems to believe he is quite seasoned. Did something happen with him? Is he safe? You look rather shocked."

His questions speared her heart. She knew what Alexander asked. Did he adhere to all the rules of safe, sane and consensual BDSM play? Yes, he did. But was he safe? Not for her. In an instant, the two years it had taken to erase every memory of his ice blue eyes, that shock of blond hair that fell across his forehead, were gone. His face crystallized in her mind as if she'd seen him last night—in the flickering red light of that basement club.

She'd been in town for London Fashion Week, and, on impulse, she'd skipped an official event. She found herself teetering down stone steps into an old wine cellar the owners had converted into a secret space. She'd seen Steffan immediately. Or he'd seen her. As she roamed by the scenes unfolding around her, his cobalt eyes had tracked her. It took less than ten minutes for him to introduce himself and invite her to co-top a red-haired woman in his care. Funny the details you remember and the ones you don't when emotions run high, like the way his lips had curved against her ear as he pressed her into that other woman they'd sent so deep into subspace—together. Steffan's eyes had shaded to violet when he stood directly under the red light that had shone down on them. She vividly pictured the desire in them when she'd said "yes" to his later proposal. A shaft of pleasure moved through her body at the memory of how they'd cele-brated their meeting later that night in his suite at the

Dorchester Hotel. Neither had topped or bottomed for the other. They'd indulged in pure, unimaginably delicious, raw, *foolish* vanilla sex.

They'd argued the next morning. He'd wanted more time with her, wanted to *get to know her*. Those were his words, right? When he'd pushed for her to stay, that cemented her decision to leave. She'd slipped out when he'd stepped out to the balcony to take a phone call. She'd left a cordial note, thanking him and did *not* leave her phone number. On the flight over the Atlantic, she'd assured herself that she could— she would—better manage herself in the future. She'd let herself go with him, broken a deal she'd made with herself decades ago. Many years before that she'd once hurt a man, deeply, but she'd recovered and made a wise, responsible, lifetime decision—all romantic liaisons would be relegated to a dungeon where protocol and rules kept everyone safe. Anything else led to dangerous consequences. She couldn't afford to be one of those women who just followed her heart and acted rashly around men. By the time she'd gotten through passport control in the States, she had thoroughly let Steffan go. She couldn't—wouldn't—have Steffan fall in love with her or her fall for him. Instead, she tucked her time with him away like a treasured souvenir from a trip to some far-off land that one places in a box under the bed. She knew it was there. She had no need to pull it out.

"Sarah?"

Her eyes snapped open, not realizing she'd disappeared so deep into memories they'd drifted closed.

"Are you sure you're all right? You know you can tell me anything."

Her chest squeezed tight at the kindness in his eyes. She had worried him, and she made a point of never worrying anyone about anything. "I'm fine." She added a slight laugh to her voice.

Alexander didn't look convinced, but she couldn't have him believe—what? Two years and she still couldn't quite nail down her feelings about what had happened, as if feelings mattered in this scenario. Steffan had *impacted* her to the point she'd let her long-held policy about men and how she got involved with them slip. In the heated darkness, she and Steffan had said things they didn't mean. They were both Dominants, for God's sake. Even if she didn't have an iron-clad rule in place around relationships, how would they ever get over *that*? A headache began like a low drumbeat behind her forehead.

"He would go through the usual vetting process," Alexander said cautiously.

"Of course, and background checks. Interviews. Tribunal Council deliberation." The mechanics kicked in quickly. She hadn't even had to think about those words. "Carson would be a good person to—"

"No, by you. It was one of Steffan's requests. He wanted you to be the one to assess his suitability and his partner's. He has a man with him."

"A man?" He was gay? A sliver of illogical hurt bubbled up that she could have been an experiment. No, Steffan's voracious sexual appetite that night with her would belie that probability. Perhaps he was bisexual, which wasn't anything new in their world. See? Already things were … messy.

"Wait until you meet Laurent. I believe you'll be intrigued. But, Sarah, if you'd rather not—"

"No, I will." Her mind had shuffled rapid-fire through decision points. Declining his request based on personal feelings would show a weakness of character that she would not allow herself. Rather, she'd alter the *significance* of his memory by recasting their roles in present time. This could be an opportunity to stuff that past experience in the bin of failed experiments. Things one did just to see what would happen. She'd be a professional with him like she was with all new potential members. He would *not* take away her control from her again.

"Good," Alexander said. "If we get started today, his thirty-day probationary status will be in place by the time the plane leaves for St. Thomas. Steffan and Laurent can join my birthday party."

"Today?" A strangled laugh died in her throat. "Wait. You want them to attend your party? You have over one hundred people on the waiting list."

"Yes and yes." Alexander smiled down at her. "They're here. In The Library."

Good-bye, relaxing weekend.

## 2

"Laurent. It's time." Steffan's lips twitched into a smile at seeing Sarah step through that overly-dramatic Gothic archway, but then the entire room was over-done. He pushed off the St. Andrew's Cross, fully intending to stride over to her but found himself pausing, allowing himself to drink in the vision of her. He was sure his memory had exaggerated her beauty. *Not at all.*

All eyes—about a dozen or so people playing or milling about—turned to her, including Laurent's. He'd been chatting up Carrie, Accendos' lead submissive assistant, after their tour of Accendos but instantly stilled at seeing Sarah. Steffan had attempted to prepare his friend for this first meeting with her, but how do you prepare someone for so much vitality—for Sarah Marillioux?

She casually gazed from one end of the room to the other, but then stopped at finding him. He grinned. Her return smile didn't reach her eyes, though a blush of pink rose in her cheeks. Well, he had taken her by surprise, and he felt something like relief that perhaps his sudden appearance might be welcomed. They'd had a rather chilly ending the last time they were together.

She glided across The Library, reaching him in four long strides, impressive given the height of her heels and the fit of her skirt. There wasn't an ounce of hesitation in her movement. It was as if they'd planned to meet today, at this time, in this place.

"Steffan. Alexander just told me you'd arrived." That silky, well-bred voice that would seduce the most hardened man hadn't changed.

"It's good to see you, Sarah." He grasped her hand and brought it to his mouth. His lips brushed her skin ever so briefly before she pulled herself free. Her perfume wafted in the air. *Baccarat Les Larmes Sacrees de Thebes*—complicated, expensive and bold like the woman who'd entered the room wearing it. He knew the scent well since he'd spent an entire evening enveloped in it. It had taken him the better part of an afternoon at Harrod's perfume counter to determine exactly what it was. Silly, but he'd wanted to know everything about her, and he was a man who pursued what intrigued him—including identifying the scent preferred by a woman like Sarah.

"This is Laurent." He gestured to his friend who had sidled up next to him.

"Miss Marillioux." Laurent bowed his head in an appropriate act of acquiescence.

"Hello, Laurent. Please call me Sarah. I look forward to getting to know you."

*I'll bet.* Steffan had noted the way her eyes raked over Laurent. The man *was* hard to ignore. A strong jaw, warm hazel eyes, and untamed dark curls he constantly had to push off forehead—all wrapped in that naturally-tanned Mediterranean skin—attracted both men and women alike.

Laurent took her outstretched hand, a slight quiver in his

fingers. For someone quite seasoned in the scene, his reaction was still warranted. Very few men would be unaffected by the energy Sarah radiated. He certainly hadn't been able to ignore it those few years ago. From the first second he'd laid eyes on her, he knew they'd be like two live wires that sparked once they touched—something he'd had the great fortune to prove two years ago. Then she'd vanished, and his life grew too complicated to force a reunion.

He still had that infuriatingly polite note with the Dorchester logo that she'd left him sitting in his safe. Saving the slip of paper was another odd thing to do but he was sure they'd had something special and he wanted that memento. If only Laurent's life hadn't imploded so spectacularly the next day he'd have tracked her down sooner. Then Amsterdam happened, and if he understood anything it was this: loyalty to friends and family eclipsed lust and desire.

She looked up at him. "Ready for your first interview?"

"Interview?"

"Yes, we have a specific protocol here at Accendos. Carrie, would you mind showing Laurent around a little? Steffan and I have some catching up to do. That is, if you don't object, Laurent."

"I'd be delighted to spend more time with Carrie." He offered his arm, which she took, looking quite pleased at this turn of events. Who could blame the girl? Laurent didn't hide his love of women, and nothing was more attractive to a woman than showing interest.

"Good," Steffan said. "I have some things to talk with you about, as well."

"Let's go to the garden." She turned on her heel.

As she marched toward the doorway, he got a terrific view of her luscious-looking backside. He'd forgotten how petite she was and his longer legs easily closed the distance between them.

"Accendos is quite formal," he said. "Is every space this ... decorated?" The velvet settees, the oil paintings, and guards at every doorway weren't something he usually saw in play spaces.

"It is." She gestured to the hallway.

"After you."

They walked silently out of The Library and into a sunny breezeway.

"I understand Alexander's gardens are also quite spectacular ..." His voice died in his throat at seeing the burst of color on the other side of several sets of glass-paned French doors leading to the back. A stone terrace spilled forward and three wide steps led down to a fountain centered in a circle of pale flagstones. A Greek statue stood in the center of the water feature.

"Pothos." She gestured to the statue and split open the middle set of doors.

"The Greek God of erotic yearning. How apropos." He stepped out into the sweet scent of flowers and wet earth. He was a man who enjoyed the small pleasures the world offered —a glass of 30-year Scotch, the curve of a woman's hip, a warm bed with his hand on that curved hip ... Given he'd spent many long Swedish winters clothed in darkness, he also had a deep appreciation of nature and sunlight. He nearly grew hypnotized by the textures, colors and designs presented and knew he'd soon spend a few hours exploring these gardens. For now, he had more pressing matters to attend to—starting with why he and Laurent were here.

Sarah didn't break her stride, stepping down the wide steps to the fountain. For long minutes they silently walked a path under a canopy of dogwood and cherry tree limbs. He had expected a warmer greeting from her, but he'd let her sit in this frigid silence until they were clear of the house. He'd wanted privacy with her anyway, and, for now, her company would be enough.

As she expertly avoided any crack or soft place where those fuck-me pumps might sink, he took the few moments to admire her. Her style hadn't wavered one bit since they'd last met, thank god. Those heels showcased her glorious legs quite well, and his cock reacted predictably to the image of her in those stilettos. Any doubts her effect on him would lessen over the years was erased.

"Laurent wasn't with you the last time I saw you." Her voice cracked the silence. "At Club 501."

"He was on the other side of the two-way glass, but back then Laurent and I weren't as we are now."

"And now?" She stopped and stared up at him, her face blank and composed.

"Now it's complicated. You look well, Sarah. I'm happy to find you here and not Morocco."

"Ah, yes, my fantasy to run away. You remembered."

It pleased him more than it should have that she laughed. Her eyes twinkled in the sunlight. They had a lighter brown center than he'd recalled. Or perhaps it was the trick of the sun. He felt a desire to squint. God, her beauty almost made his eyes hurt. "I remember everything."

She made a small dismissive sound and resumed walking. They stopped at a smaller fountain, this one graced by a statue of Venus holding an urn tipped to the side. Water spilled from its lip. Sarah silently studied the woman's face, her profile mirroring the perfection of the marble goddess. How many men had gawped at her like he did now, wishing to fall at her feet or be the one to stand by her side? Legions, he imagined. He hadn't noticed a wedding ring, but then Sarah wouldn't succumb to anything that equaled ownership. She could not be possessed, a quality he admired. He had no need for possession of anyone or anything either. He enjoyed control but not ownership.

"I'm surprised you're not in Sweden, the place you said you'd never leave."

"Yes, well, things changed. Sweden will always be my home. Washington holds more promise now. I've launched a new nonprofit, Water Wise. We fund clean water projects. I'm here to raise awareness and make the fund-raising rounds."

"Really?"

"Water is so vital to life, so taken for granted. There are more people on this planet who don't have access to clean water than those who do. It's unconscionable."

"And you'll change that." Her words were crisp, and an understanding bloomed in his chest. He knew that letting so much time pass between them could have been a tactical error, despite the fact it was for a good reason. Sarah also wasn't an ordinary woman—someone who pined over a man not calling, and she hadn't left her number. Finding her, however, hadn't been difficult once he made up his mind about doing so. While his visit was unexpected, he'd rather hoped it would be received as a good surprise, and that it would at least get him an audience.

She began to circle the fountain, never taking her eyes off the statute. The woman radiated unease, which troubled him.

"I'm going to try to change a great many things. Sarah, I apologize for not warning you about my appearance, and I realize it's been a long time, but I had believed we parted as friends. Did we?"

"We did," she said. "And yes, it has been a long time. So … you wish to join Club Accendos."

"Yes, and I'd like to explain what happened two years ago."

"You don't need to."

"I do. It has to do with Laurent."

"You're lovers."

He was used to people believing such a thing. "No, we're not."

She stopped short and blinked at him. Her formal tone had begun to irritate him. While they hadn't seen one another in two years, they *had* seen every inch of each other's bodies the last time they were together.

"We're best friends," he said. "Have been since birth. Our mothers were in the hospital together. We were born six hours apart. Laurent's mother was new to Sweden, an immigrant, single, and my mother's heart went out to her."

She'd resumed her pacing, though had her head cocked as if listening intently. He walked with her and moved a branch that threatened her shoulder.

"We are very close, Laurent and I. The day after our weekend together, he lost his mother and stepfather in a car accident …" Once more she halted her progress. Her eyes softened, filled with compassion. Ah, that was the warm fire he remembered—a natural, fierce protective energy that she emanated. He'd picked up on it when they'd played together, her desire to make sure everyone around her was safe.

"I've very sorry to hear that."

"He didn't handle it well. They were his only family other than me."

"Close but not lovers." She seemed to be mulling her words in her mind.

"No. We share women sometimes." That was the wrong thing to say. Her eyes shot to his face, the frost in them returning. Could she be jealous? Wishful thinking on his part but his ego didn't mind having a bone thrown to it now and again. Believing Sarah cared who he slept with was one very nice, juicy bone.

"But"—he continued—"for Laurent … men, women, it

doesn't matter to him. He's the most democratic human being I've ever met. He would never dismiss someone because of gender."

"And, you?"

"Women only. I'm not here to discuss me, however. I'm here for Laurent." It wasn't exactly true, but first, he had to get her to understand the last two years. How did he explain this next part without betraying Laurent's privacy—or losing his temper? What happened to his friend made him want to punch a wall. "His needs have grown. He started seeking others. A little over a year ago, a fetish group lured him to Amsterdam. There was alcohol abuse. Drugs. A shocking lack of consent." His ability to articulate what happened died. Thinking about Laurent in that house where he'd found him made his teeth clench so hard they might shatter.

"Who was it?" God, he loved her in that second for the fierce tone she adopted. Instantly, they were connected again in a shared need to protect and serve those who gave of themselves so freely like Laurent, like that redhead that night.

"I will let him tell you, but know that it's been handled." He glanced down at his right hand. He wasn't a violent man, but he'd forever carry that scar on his right knuckle with pride. He'd punched the black-hooded man who'd refused to let him see Laurent when he'd arrived at that shit hole. He was 100 percent okay with both his actions and the permanent mark.

He sighed heavily. "That situation showed me he needs someone watching out for him, more than I can. He finally admitted he's seeking a … belonging. He's someone who, as you Americans say, is *all in.*" He took a deep breath. "So, a few months ago, when I first raised coming here, he specifically asked if *you*—"

ELIZABETH SAFLEUR

"Me?" Her voice was laced with incredulity. "I'm not looking for someone."

Of course she wasn't. Sarah's desire to remain unattached was well-established and one of the reasons he had let her get on that plane two years ago despite his instincts to run after her. Sarah had made it clear she had not required him with that cold note she'd left. Now, seeing her in those sky-high heels and wrapped in that confidence ratcheted up that simmering desire he'd kept banked for her. Why not test the possibility of them picking up where they'd left off?

"How about two someones? Both Laurent and I." He closed the distance between them, taking in her captivating scent again. "We were good together that night, weren't we? I can still see you in that midnight blue velvet dress, and those"—his eyes raked down her torso and her legs to her feet—"death heels."

She laughed. "Death heels?"

"I still can't get over how you could yield a bull whip in those shoes and in that tiny space." Shit, he was getting a hard-on just thinking about their scene, their private after-party.

"I think I cleared the room."

"No one would have dared leave. No one would miss their chance to see you work. I wouldn't."

She gazed up at him, and he had a curious desire to press his lips where a wisp of hair curled on her neck.

"So, that's why you're here? To relive that night?"

"I'm not sure that's possible." How could perfection be topped?

"My thoughts exactly." That ice returned to her eyes, and in them, a truth. She considered their time had passed, an idea he vehemently rejected. They'd spent one glorious weekend, co-topping and then continuing their appreciation for the human form in bed—just the two of them. Hell, yeah, his cock thickened thinking of her under him, on top of him, so many ways … However, he would let her believe their time together was over—for now. Something more important was at stake. He straightened.

"Laurent needs you, Sarah. I wouldn't trust him with anyone else. He's incapable of seeing himself clearly. His need to serve overtakes his sense of self-preservation."

"Dangerous."

"Yes. I won't be easy in my mind until I know he has someone who can give him everything he requires, including protection."

She crossed her arms. "Let me get this straight. You're offering Laurent to me."

"He's not mine to offer, only he can do that, but he needs your touch. Know this … so long as Laurent is here, I will be here."

She laughed and dropped her arms. "My touch? You wish me to play with him so he *also* can say he spent time with me?"

A flash of white-hot anger rushed up his spine. "How very arrogant of you. Nothing could be further from the truth. I didn't use you then, and I don't intend to use you now." He pressed forward until a bare inch separated them. "I very much enjoyed our weekend together, Sarah. I wasn't the only one who didn't send a Christmas card."

"Touché," she whispered.

He scrubbed his chin. "At least speak with Laurent. Judge for yourself."

"I'll speak with him next, but alone. For one thing, I want to know who this group was."

"Like I said, I handled it, but feel free to ask him." He stepped backward, more to give himself a break from inhaling that perfume that was driving him crazy.

"I will." She pivoted on her heels giving him yet another

glorious view of her ass. "Enjoy the gardens while I'm inside. It's not often so much is blooming at once—and no promises, Steffan," she said without looking back.

*Yes, because we're good at that, aren't we?* She'd gotten on that plane years ago with no talk of staying in touch—and he'd let her. It didn't matter now. So what if he'd made a mistake allowing such distance between them. What mattered now was that he make no more. He had her, and then he'd lost her—for a good reason, but he'd lost her, nonetheless. So what if he'd miscalculated the impact she'd still have on him. Jesus, the way her ass moved in those heels ... The first time he'd seen her, she'd summoned a roaring hunger in him. He'd wanted her beyond logical thought, hell, still did. She, however, seemed fine without him. If he couldn't change that fact, he'd live with it. He'd live with it for Laurent.

# 3

Sarah paused inside the doorway of the submissives' lounge. All thoughts of the ache in her feet or the sudden appearance of Steffan in that finely-cut European suit vanished at the sight of Laurent and Carrie together on the longest of the two black, velvet-covered couches.

Laurent bent closer to Carrie's ear and whispered something. They sat so close their knees touched. From the intimate bend of his neck toward her, the way his eyes remained riveted to her face, if Sarah hadn't known they'd just met, she would have guessed they were lovers. He said something. Carrie flushed. So this was the man who wanted her to dominate him. After seeing her behind a pane of glass? *Curious.* Steffan was going to stick around and perhaps wanted in on it? *Disconcerting.* A group of abusers had lured Laurent? *Enraging.* She'd get to the bottom of that last one—soon.

"Hello, Laurent," Sarah said softly.

He turned calmly and gave her a smile. "Mistress." He stood giving her a full view of his well-proportioned chest. It was then she noticed Carrie's hand attached to his. The young girl darted up and dropped his hand.

ELIZABETH SAFLEUR

"Thank you, Carrie," she said. "Laurent and I need to talk."

"Mistress Sarah." Before the girl could scoot by, Sarah gave her a reassuring squeeze on her arm. She'd done nothing wrong, and by the looks of Laurent, he had much practice seducing women. Carrie simply dipped her head and strode out.

"I'd like to speak with you privately."

"Whatever you wish, Mistress." For the second time today, a man presented his elbow for her to take. Most men in her sphere hadn't let their formal manners slip—thank god—but the way Laurent offered his arm, with his head bowed and eyes downcast, she nearly melted. She hooked her hand over his bicep and let a small fantasy build—of him on his knees before her, a riding crop in her hand.

"What did Carrie show you?" she asked.

"She brought me here right away. She said you might wish to show me around yourself."

She'd tell Alexander to give that girl a raise.

"So you haven't seen the Masters' private library yet?" Aside from each Tribunal member's private bedroom, the hidden library was the most private spot in Accendos.

"I didn't know there was one."

"Then that's where we'll start."

"Whatever pleases you." *Melt, indeed.* They stepped out into the hallway.

"Laurent, here at Accendos, you don't acquiesce to anything you don't want to do. It doesn't matter who is asking. You can ask me to show you the gardens instead or anywhere else. And, call me Sarah for now."

His warm eyes met hers, flashing green and gold. "Sarah."

She rather liked hearing her name on those full lips. "Good. It's important we get to know one another as people before anything else can occur."

"Where's Steffan?"

"Enjoying the garden."

"I believe it. He loves being outside." He laughed softly.

"He told me about your family's loss. I am so sorry."

"Thank you." His eyes lowered and then moved across the oil paintings they passed in the hall. "This is quite the place. Very different from other places I've been."

"You will find a great many things different at any place Alexander is involved with. I understand you were with some people in Amsterdam. Who?"

He chuckled. "He told you, huh? Steffan is protective."

"He's a good Dom."

"He says you're better."

She doubted that given the size of the ego she'd just encountered. "That wouldn't be wholly true. Let's say we're equals, but, we don't suffer fools in our realm. If Steffan had concerns over someone, then I have to report it."

"Honestly, we weren't together that long. It was a small fetish group. They called themselves the Masters of X."

*Oh, Jesus.* She stifled a laugh. Someone had been reading too much BDSM fiction, and not the good kind. She'd tell Alexander. He would ferret out the mysterious Masters of X.

They strode through The Library's grand doors. Laurent paused before a stern-looking Mistress Seraphina and a man on his knees that Sarah didn't recognize. Carrie knelt next to him, his cock in her hand, her eyes downcast. None of them paid any attention to the fact they had an audience. Sarah recognized the moment as a punishment.

She turned her eyes to Laurent whose eyes locked onto the scene. "What do you think he's done?" she whispered.

"Displeased her." Beautiful color glowed in Laurent's cheeks and his hazel eyes filled with longing. "Having another submissive hold his cock when all he wants is his Mistress's touch is a reprimand." Laurent's voice was hushed, reverent.

That answer pleased *her* to her core. She dropped her hold on his arm and held out her palm. "Take my hand," she said.

He engulfed her smaller hand in his, the heat and softness instantly sending a pang to between her legs. She loved so many things about men—their single-mindedness, the hardness of their bodies, and their size, everything larger than her. Yet she prized their strength the most. When they submitted to her, these creatures who could easily overpower her but chose not to, it fed both her own power and her sense of purpose.

Hand in hand, she and Laurent climbed the circular staircase that led to the gallery down which was the door to the Masters' private library.

Once through the door, Laurent paused in awe. "I never would have guessed this was here."

"Yes, it's tucked away like a secret."

He pointed to the fireplace stacked with wood, ready for a fire. "Would you like me to light that? I was a pretty good scout growing up."

"Not now. Come sit with me." She took one of the two, large leather chairs before the fireplace and crossed her legs.

He'd tried to sink to his knees, but she stopped him. She patted the seat across from her. He might not be comfortable being at eye level with her, but the more equal position was necessary. She wasn't taking him on—yet.

"Now, I understand you wanted to meet me?"

"Oh yes." He swallowed. "I understand you don't have someone … and I might be able to help with that."

She'd heard this offer countless times. "I'm not seeking anyone permanent right now, but—"

"Why not? Oh, sorry." He lowered his gaze. "That was impertinent." The urge to drop to his knees poured out of his pores. His hands curled over the edge of the stiff cushion, his eyes studying the carpet pattern.

"Kneel for me."

His long lashes flicked up and then immediately down to the floor at her sudden command. He sank to his knees, and a sense of wishing to protect this strong yet vulnerable creature soared through her. Was her sudden need to watch over him truly because of him? She barely knew this man. Perhaps she just had some banked desires itching to get out. She had been working a lot lately.

"Your English is quite good." His speech tinged with a Spanish accent added to his allure.

"Thank you. Everyone in Sweden learns English. I also speak Catalan. It was my mother's native tongue."

The sadness on his face wrenched her heart. "That will be very useful here. Alexander enjoys an international crowd." She placed the pointed tip of her shoe under his chin and raised his face. "Laurent, what do you need?"

"May I do something for you?" he asked.

"And what would that be?" She lowered her foot.

"Nice Valentino's." He said without hesitation and traced a fingertip alongside the arch of her pump. "May I give you a foot massage?"

"You may."

He slipped her foot from her shoe. "Elegant feet."

*Flatterer.* Except the sincerity in his face couldn't be denied not to mention the strength in his thumb as he kneaded her arch. He pulled on her toes one by one.

"Mmmm, I like that." Forget a lavender bath. She could sit in this chair having him do *that* for an hour.

"I have a confession to make," he said.

"Oh?"

After he placed her foot on his thigh, he liberated her

other one from her shoe. "I saw you a second time at Club 501. Last year. I wasn't with Steffan."

"Why you didn't come and say hello?" It had been unwise for her to stop in to the Club, but she'd felt compelled to revisit for some odd reason. She chalked it up to her need to prove she had no lingering effects of her previous encounter there.

"I would never. I would wait to be introduced properly."

She smiled at his formality. Oh, this man was either incredibly perceptive or truly sincere. She'd take either. Very few subs were anticipatory anymore. *So many brats in our world.*

"May I tell you why I wanted to meet you now?"

"I'm interested in everything you have to say, Laurent."

"Steffan trusts you. I had never seen him play with another before ... that night." They both knew which night he referenced, which thanks to Steffan's ambush, showing up here unannounced, she couldn't stop thinking about.

She leaned back into the hard leather cushion and fought the urge to close her eyes. His fingers were magic. "Were you jealous?"

"No. I was privileged. You and Steffan were good together. I realized how I'd been gifted with watching two of the best people one could know in our world. I'd be honored to be a part of your life in any capacity you see fit. Time slips away so quickly, and I don't believe in wasting any more of it. If you really think about it, our lives are so short."

Were they? Contrary to what most believed, she'd always felt time crept along. The only time it didn't was when she scened. Then time suspended. She wouldn't mind suspending a little of it with this gorgeous creature. His face resembled one of the cherub statues that Alexander had outside in his gardens—angular cheekbones without being hard, inviting full lips, a head of tousled curls. If a man could be called lovely, he would be.

"Would you like to scene with me? Alone?" Her own words shocked her, but he looked so ... accessible—yes, that was the word—kneeling at her feet, his hands removing all tension from her ankle to her toes. What was the harm, really, in exploring the possibility?

His answering smile warmed her head to foot.

"Yes, I will consider you, Laurent," she answered his unspoken question. "So long as you understand, I can only offer you a temporary situation."

"I'd take anything you wish to offer, Mistress Sarah."

"Anything?"

"I don't believe in depriving oneself. It would be my honor to submit to you, to give you whatever you require for as long as you need."

She sighed. "Steffan mentioned you weren't good at setting limits for yourself."

"I believe in fulfilling my purpose. Mine is to serve, and I know who I wish to serve."

No wonder Steffan couldn't bear to be left out. If Laurent had been hers, she wouldn't have allowed him to cross the street without her. His willingness was endearing but also dangerous. Talk about catnip to an unscrupulous Dom, and there had been far too many of those cropping up lately. Perhaps, temporarily, she could help this man who seemed borderline desperate to belong to someone. Laurent could also help her move past this sudden Steffan sighting. Steffan's appearance in that gorgeous suit should not have rattled her to this extent, despite the memories he'd unearthed, despite his invasion into her weekend plans. Scening with the handsome sub could be an admirable diversion and derail any lingering doubts about her decision to put her time with Steffan behind her. She could redirect this whole situation. With that thought, her composure returned. Not difficult at all.

She pulled her foot free and stood. "You can rise. I'll escort you back to Carrie who will help you find Steffan. Seraphina is probably done by now. She's quick. I'll think about your offer and talk with Steffan, see if he's willing to observe."

"I believe he'd do anything you asked."

She chuffed. "We'll see."

She was about to ask the man to sit on the sidelines, not a natural environment for someone as dominant as Steffan—but he had asked to be involved. *How about two someones?* Okay, she'd let him watch, but that was it. She'd let her control slip that fateful weekend with him, acted like any other normal, hot-blooded woman. Now, she felt her resolve weaken once more in his presence—and that would never do.

She'd worked hard to design her life, not be pulled in whatever direction life threw at her. She had everything she needed—a profession she adored, wonderful friends and Club Accendos when she needed to burnish off the edge. The price for such freedom was having occasional bouts of loneliness, and she had male subs lined up, waiting for her interest. Right now, the one before her made that persistent hollow feeling lessen a bit. That alone meant something, and she'd explore—on her terms, with rules and procedures in place. They'd be vetted as new Accendos members, she might play a little with Laurent, and no one would get hurt—not on her watch. Decision made, she slipped her feet free of Laurent's care.

Returning to The Library, she left him with Carrie. She caught sight of Steffan still in the garden as she strode through the breezeway to Alexander's office. He stood with his back to her, staring up at the statue of Pothos. Steffan was taller than she recalled. He turned suddenly and caught her gawking at him. He smiled and dipped his head but made no move to come to her. For long minutes she stood there, his striking blue eyes holding her in place with an unblinking stare. She had to force herself to breathe. Empirically, he was handsome, different from Laurent, but beautiful nonetheless.

When she finally did rip her attention away, instead of heading to Alexander, she turned to head to her room. If she hadn't needed a long soak in a tub before, she certainly did now. Perhaps the warm water would melt away her memories of Steffan *out* of his suit. Despite her decision to right the balance between them, she didn't lie to herself. He could impact her again. She was going to have to shore up her defenses, starting with retreating to her room to think, to plan, to *strategize*.

# 4

---

Laurent leaned back on the park bench overlooking the Potomac and sipped his cappuccino. The homeless man at the other end of the bench eyed him suspiciously but stuck his grimy hand in the bag Laurent had handed him anyway. No way would Laurent eat a pastry in front of someone who desperately needed help. Besides, he didn't know many people in DC yet, and the guy seemed as good as any to talk about the dark-haired mistress he couldn't get out of his mind.

"Her name is Sarah," he told the man.

The man grunted and stuffed the croissant he found between his lips—or Laurent thought so. Who could tell with all that gray and yellow facial hair spiking in all directions?

"Means princess." Crumbs blew out of the man's mouth. The guy brushed at his tattered pants.

"It fits." The meaning did fit. The woman didn't have an ounce of diva in her, but she certainly presented quite the package. That perfectly tailored white blouse tucked into a pencil skirt, those torturous Valentino pumps, her hair pulled back into a long cascade of chestnut waves, it all created the vision of someone who understood how to present herself powerfully. He understood Steffan's inability to take his eyes off her, and how she would appeal to him.

Laurent unscrewed the top of his small Evian bottle and handed it to the guy who greedily drained it.

"Bless you," the man said before rising and toddling off to god knew where, his maniac mutterings trailing behind him.

*There I am but for the grace of God.* Watching him stumble to evade other pedestrians, Laurent almost jumped up to force the man in the direction of the homeless shelter he'd passed earlier. Steffan's voice echoed annoyingly in his head. *Let go.*

Laurent sighed. "So many people with money here and they still can't figure this one out."

He'd counted the number of homeless in the park— thirty-six men and women. If Steffan hadn't intervened, he could have been living on the street himself, and now he paid close attention to those wanting. He glanced down at his watch. He had an hour to kill before meeting Steffan and the realtor to look at yet another house in DC they might buy. He'd convinced Steffan that purchasing a place was better than renting. He wasn't so sure that one year was going to be enough time here for any of them. Sarah proved more suspicious of them than he'd expected.

He closed his eyes and fixed his mind on thoughts of that dark-haired woman he'd hoped—no, prayed—he could call his Mistress. When he first saw her at Accendos, he'd been trying to help Carrie with some advice. She strode into the room with such confidence the urge to fall to his knees and beg her to accept his service sprang up so hard he'd nearly done it. Serving her, pleasing her, would require ultimate submission, something that turned him on, body and soul. He wasn't the only one affected by her presence. Steffan didn't have a submissive element to his personality, but

Laurent noted his friend's strong reaction to her. He watched her with a lust-filled reverence he'd never before seen in the man's eyes. Steffan's desire for her hadn't waned one bit since Laurent had been riveted by them co-topping that redhead. Days later, he'd asked Steffan about her, wanting to know what about her had intrigued him enough to play with such a powerful Domme.

"She's my equal," he'd said. "Or I'm hers."

That wasn't a small thing for Steffan to admit. He loved his friend, but Steffan had an arrogant streak as wide as the river he now stared at. Yet Steffan had let Sarah slip away. *Because of me.* Steffan and his honor, he thought ruefully. It rivaled his self-confidence. The man really did need to learn to multi-task.

Laurent inhaled a lungful of air scented with auto fumes, briny river water, and tacos from a Mexican food truck down the river walk. It did little to tamp down his memory of Sarah's perfume—of her entire erotic package for that matter. How did any man *not* want in her life? So polished, so beautiful, so intelligent, so … everything.

His mind whirled with things he could do for her. She looked tired, but not the kind that one good night's sleep would take care of. No, she needed taking care of, period. If only she'd let him. He loved serving women, making sure they didn't overextend themselves, which they always did. Service was the ultimate soul boost for him. Without someone to help, his self-worth didn't just take a hit—it plummeted.

He had a sixth sense about people—a radar for who needed him. Sarah needed … something. Of course, his radar had been a tad banged up in recent years. Still, she seemed so isolated. He pushed down that ache that thrummed in his chest when he thought how alone people really were in the world. If they only knew how much helping others was the answer they sought from all those shopping trips, yoga retreats, and books on happiness that people devoured. He understood the temporary boost of an Armani suit or a circle of diamonds around a finger, but it didn't make a life.

He never wanted anyone to suffer the self-destructive despair that haunted him when loneliness and a lack of purpose overtook him. He was grateful for his unwavering friendship with Steffan, but Laurent needed more, a Mistress and that one-on-one interaction when you evoked her entire regard. He was certain Sarah could be the one. He also believed she could be the one for Steffan.

He rose. Time to stroll through the crowded streets of Georgetown to the townhome he and Steffan might buy. There was time enough to explore how he might make more inroads with Sarah, the first step in his plan. She seemed willing to at least consider him. Right now, he couldn't ask for more. He'd fallen too deeply into himself over the last few years—made some bad choices. He and Steffan both had, so it was time to set them all on a new course, one that sustained all three of them.

# 5

Steffan stepped into the slash of sunshine that cut across the hardwood floors of the vacant living room and pointed to the fireplace.

"Works?" he asked the leggy blonde realtor.

"Absolutely. There are a few cords of wood in the back that convey." She leaned against the fireplace and crossed one slim ankle over the other. "Where did you say you were from again?" She cocked her head. She'd been eyeing him from the second they shook hands in front of the For Sale sign outside.

"Stockholm. I hear DC winters are mostly slush and rain."

"Oh, we get the odd snowfall. It shuts the city down. Nothing left for you and Laurent to do but curl up before a fire."

Ah, she'd been trying to figure out if he was gay. He was used to people assuming he and Laurent were lovers. It didn't matter to him if she knew the truth or not.

"Unless you have a girlfriend …" Her lips curled into a coy smile.

Laurent's horse-clomp footsteps sounded above him.

"Hardwoods above?" He pointed to the ceiling. Noisy, but they could be charming if they'd been finished as nicely as the ones on which he now stood.

"Yes, I could show you—"

"Score!" Laurent called from upstairs. "You were right, Penelope. Unexpectedly good closet space for an old house."

"You and your clothes," he called up as he headed toward the kitchen. *Score, indeed*. He paused in the arched doorway.

"Stainless steel appliances, quartz counter-tops," Penelope said behind him.

A large island that could seat four people sat in the center and anchored his decision. They were moving in as soon as possible. Hotel rooms and restaurants were depressing.

She squeezed by him in the doorway—slowly. Her breasts brushed against his arm. "Oh, excuse me," she said.

If all women in DC were going to be this forthcoming, he was going to have to consider spreading a few untrue rumors about himself and Laurent. Women were bold in Sweden but paled to what he'd encountered to date here.

A quick glance out the window showed an endless stream of BMWs and Audis passing by on the narrow one-way, tree-lined street.

"Parking?" he asked.

"Two parking spaces in back. So unusual for this neighborhood. I expect this property will be snatched up today, so—"

"Well, can we?" Laurent's jubilant voice broke into the room.

"We can." He turned to Penelope. "We'll take it."

"Excellent. I'll draw up the contract later this morning and break open the champagne."

Laurent scanned the kitchen. "I guess we're going to Kitchen Emporium for more appliances? I know you can't stand empty counter space. Plus, you need to dazzle Sarah with your cooking skills."

Penelope's face fell. "I'll call you later once everything's in order."

"Thank you," Laurent said. "May I walk you to your car?"

"Oh, that would be wonderful." Now free of her affections, Laurent could deal with her. Laurent winked at him before following Penelope out.

Laurent didn't usually play interference, but Steffan welcomed it today. He wasn't in the mood for flirtations, not when he had so much to settle in coming weeks—for Water Wise, for Laurent, for their lives here. He wasn't sure a year was going to do it now, faced with a dawning reality of Washington, DC. Everyone moved so quickly yet did anything really progress? He'd expected Accendos to have a vetting process, but Jesus …

A courier had dropped off a set of forms to their hotel that would rival the merger of two banks, though the questions they asked on their questionnaires were far more interesting. Medical background, mandatory STD tests, hard limits, soft limits, instruments preferred, references … the list of what they required made his head spin. Then, there was the hefty annual fee for the privilege of baring one's sexual soul. In addition to Sarah and Alexander, the other five Tribunal Council members—Derek and the others he hadn't yet met, Jonathan Brond, Ryan Knightbridge, Carson Drake and Marcos Santos—would soon know everything about him and Laurent. He supposed that's why Alexander's band of merry Dominants were known as the best in the scene, never allowing abusers in their midst. Thank god. He'd had enough of those.

Steffan strode to the slider and stepped out onto a small terrace littered with sticks and white cherry blossoms.

Alexander answered on the second ring. "Steffan."

"Alexander. Catching you a bad time?"

"Not at all. I trust our membership package arrived today."

"Yes, you'll have it back by tomorrow. I'd also like to thank you for allowing Laurent and I to be at Accendos these past few days even though we're not members." He and Laurent had the full tour—a house even larger on the inside than the outside projected—and been allowed to observe the play of others. Without a Tribunal Council member in attendance or formal permission from Alexander, they were still forbidden to play themselves.

"You can thank Sarah for that," Alexander said. "She suggested you and Laurent come to Charlotte's collaring ceremony—if we can get your probationary status in order."

Oh, really? Sarah certainly was taking her time filling him in.

"I'm afraid I haven't met Charlotte. Are you sure?"

"All members are invited. It will still be an intimate gathering with a small after-party," Alexander continued. "I trust you'd be interested?"

"Wouldn't miss it."

"Why don't you come around to lunch, say Wednesday at noon? That suit your schedule?"

Steffan knew enough about Accendos that turning down Alexander wasn't an option, and at least it meant something was moving forward. He itched to get established. "Perfect."

It was more than perfect. He had some questions of his own—about Sarah. Something wasn't quite right. She had a rigidity he hadn't experienced from her before. She'd grown … armored. Then again, what did he really know about her other than she moaned deliciously during orgasm and her attention to rules and protocols rivaled the Queen of England?

He killed the call and returned inside to find Laurent sitting on the island.

"Has Sarah called you?" Laurent sounded so eager. He didn't blame him. Steffan wanted to see her again, too.

"No. How was your interview with her?"

"Interesting. I think she'd love your cinnamon buns. We should do brunch … here." Laurent swept his arms wide over the island.

"No details, hmm? Well, your interview is your business."

Laurent gave him one of his lop-sided smiles that had charmed the pants off hundreds of women—and men. "She's going to ask you if it's okay for us to move forward. She wants to play." He averted his eyes.

"What do you want?"

"I want to explore all three of us together. She seems to want to play alone, however."

"Of course she does." He had badly miscalculated a few things—first, making their appearance a surprise and second, assuming they could pick up where they left off. Her ambivalence toward him didn't dampen her appeal, however, which annoyed. He wasn't one to run after anyone.

"You're okay with this, right? I mean you two did have a thing," Laurent said.

"Of course." He'd get over her refusal to co-top. "You get your school application in?" Laurent was going for his degree in physical therapy and classes started soon. Laurent needed to be occupied, or he'd go nuts.

"Signed, sealed, delivered."

"Good, listen, I have another call to make. Start ordering furniture. I know you're dying to."

He hopped off the counter. "On it."

Steffan fingered his phone. What the hell. Waiting wasn't his style. He dialed Sarah's number, and it immediately went to voice mail.

"Sarah, checking in," he said into her mailbox. "Give me a call." He wouldn't betray Laurent's confidence, but he wouldn't betray his own common sense, either. Despite her obvious dismissal of him, he needed to know what she was up to. She was going to talk with him, but playing alone with Laurent? She hadn't mentioned that to him, and she should have. So, *no*, not until she revealed her desires and plans more directly. If she was considering Laurent, he had to know she understood the depth of Laurent's longings to be of use, to belong, not to mention his reckless neglect of his own safety. Sure, Laurent was better now—less apt to self-harm from his excessive need to serve—but he could fall in love and then what? Another deep loss could cripple his friend. He knew first-hand how Sarah's attention could spellbind a man. Hell, he felt that tug toward her now despite her rebuffs. Then again when had that ever stopped him from going after what he wanted? He hadn't amassed his philanthropic-bound fortune without taking risks. None of those involved his heart so directly, however. Shit, he was going to have to tread carefully around this unfolding scenario—starting with getting more information on the motivations of a woman he couldn't stop thinking about.

# 6

Sarah tapped her foot. The barista moved slowly today. Sarah had an hour before her next appointment, but her need for caffeine this morning eclipsed any patience she could muster. Thanks to another restless evening, she'd never live through another of Christiana's bridal gown fittings un-caffeinated. She'd woken up three times from dreams, fantasies about Laurent and a certain Swede.

"She did what?" Jonathan, her stepbrother, stepped through the door of the coffee shop, his familiar voice turning heads as he barked into his phone. He was hard to ignore given his fame in this town.

He lifted his chin at her.

"Coffee?" she mouthed and pointed to the counter.

"Please," he mouthed back. He inclined his head to an empty table and took a seat. Finally making it to the head of the line, she retrieved their usual orders—espresso for her and cappuccino for Jonathan, and lowered herself across from him. He spun his cell phone with his finger on the table top.

"Having a bad day?" she asked.

He scrubbed his chin. "Things have been a little tense at home."

"What has my mother done now?" Claire Marillioux Brond had married Jonathan's father when they were both young, and the woman could not stop interfering in Jonathan's life, especially since her stepbrother was having what her mother had declared the "wedding of the century." The fact that Sarah was still single, which has been Claire's greatest life disappointment to date, was also a factor.

"What *hasn't* she done? She's taken over an event Christiana never wanted in the first place. Now Christiana is talking about postponing again … I mean, Christ, we're three months out …"

"She'll marry you, Jay." She placed her hand on his wrist. She'd added more older-sister vibe in her tone than she'd meant, but his nervousness wasn't merited. "She's doing what the very young do, questioning everything."

*And being intimidated by my steam-roller mother.* Jonathan, the golden boy of Washington, had fallen for one of the "common people" and had given up his seat in Congress for Christiana. Washington, D.C. didn't trust true love—neither its existence nor its ability to stick. Rather, they lined up waiting for the impending train wreck. More than most, she wholly understood their suspicion, but this was her stepbrother, whom she loved more than life.

"I get it. She wants to explore the world before tying herself down, but it has been three years." He took a large gulp of his drink, wincing at the heat.

"Jay, why have a wedding at all? I've never seen a woman so in love as Christiana is with you. Elope."

"She might regret not having a wedding later, and I won't allow Claire to ruin if for her. Someday you'll understand."

"I doubt that." She'd never don a wedding gown or tie herself to one man.

"Sarah." Jonathan's tone softened, and he drew a breath to speak.

"Stop. Don't," she warned. He wisely took a sip of his coffee instead. Jonathan was one of the few people in the world who knew *how and why* she'd become whom she was today—how she'd carefully crafted her life after ... well, just after. She'd learned her lesson well.

"How goes it with the new male sub, Laurent?" Jonathan asked. "Yes, Derek filled me in."

Glad of the change of subject, she responded with a roll of the eyes, "Of course he did. Well, I'm about to find out. Laurent's offered himself. Nearly begged, actually."

"Begged? Already he knows the way to your heart. And, the other new guy. Steffan? How goes it with him?"

"Fine, I suppose. I haven't seen him since Alexander asked me to do the initial interview." His curt voice mail an hour ago didn't count.

He eyed her. "I ran into Steffan in the hallway. Said he was pleased to finally meet Sarah's brother. Made me wonder if you two knew each other."

"We've met before."

"Anything I need to know before Tribunal Council deliberations?" His eyebrow arched.

"Just the usual arrogance and control issues."

"Stop talking about me."

She chuckled. Jonathan always could make her laugh. She finished her espresso and rose. "Love you, Jay. Now, I must go do battle with my mother so you may have the wedding of your dreams." She pecked him on the cheek.

"You sure you're okay, Sarah?" He grabbed her wrist stopping her and gave her a searching look.

"I'm fine." She hated worrying him. She slipped from his hold and smiled. "I didn't sleep well last night. See you at the Tribunal Council meeting, if not before." After the meeting, she'd return Steffan's call. She needed time to consider Laurent's desires and her own. Their parachute into Washington with an intriguing, albeit, disconcerting offer required careful maneuvering. She also refused to be forced to choose before she was ready *or* taken down some garden path she didn't agree to. No, this situation required all her strategic thinking before it turned into a predicament.

She'd always been comfortable with her power—and known how it could be the undoing of others if she weren't careful. Laurent's face sprang up in her mind—and Steffan's warning. *His need to serve overtakes his sense of self-preservation.* Well, not if she had anything to do with it.

As soon as she stepped outside, her cell phone rang.

"Hi, Yvette. Don't tell me you're bailing on the dress fitting." Her best female friend and one of Christiana's bridesmaids had a way with her mother, soothing and appeasing her in a way Sarah never had been able to. Sarah and her mother were like gasoline meeting a brushfire.

"I would never. You need reinforcements. No, I'm calling to make sure you're coming to my event tonight."

"Why?"

"Someone asked to sit next to you, and I know how you hate surprises. Steffan Vidar? He says you're old friends."

"My, how the man gets around," she muttered under her breath. Yvette was the most successful fundraising consultant in Washington. Of course, he'd find his way to her.

"Yvette, I'll be at my fitting studio in five minutes. We'll talk then." She killed the call, prayed her new car lived up to its reputation for speed, and that her mother was late.

Jesus, so much for deep thinking. Why had Steffan asked to sit next to her at Yvette's fundraising dinner? How had he known she was even going? If he could find her schedule, he certainly could have found her phone number and warned her he was in town. He either wanted her unsettled or he'd been afraid she'd say "no" to talking with him? She dismissed the latter. Steffan didn't seem to be the type of man who was afraid of much. She concluded he wanted her off guard. *How cute.* He would be sorely disappointed then.

First, however, she had to have an awkward conversation with Yvette. She'd never told her about Steffan, and she didn't want to now—especially since she had a countermove to plan. However, perhaps Yvette could help. The answer was so easy she laughed aloud at herself. She knew *exactly* what to do. The answer to sitting next to her? *No.* She had something better in mind.

# 7

---

"Hmmm, I think it's a little too ... revealing." Her mother frowned. Claire walked a wide circle around Christiana who fidgeted like she'd rather be anywhere else than standing on a podium before a three-way mirror in Sarah's styling studio. Her mother, as usual, was oblivious to her pending daughter-in-law's discomfort.

Sarah shot Yvette a silent appeal. The coward shook her head slightly and mouthed, "You're on your own." When Sarah arrived, her mother was already there bossing her assistant around like she owned the place. Yvette arrived shortly after, so her conversation about Steffan would have to wait until the coast was clear.

Christiana pulled on the bodice of the wedding dress. "Why is everything so form-fitting these days?"

"It's beautiful on you." Sarah straightened the train. She was right. The dress would have Jonathan's eyes popping from his head, but the elegance of the sleek mermaid-style gown would be lost if Christiana didn't stop fussing.

The young girl sighed heavily and then frowned. "See? I

can't breathe in this thing. I mean, Sarah …" Christiana gave Sarah a withering look.

She had never met a woman so in love yet so uninterested in a march down a wedding aisle as Christiana Snow. Well, except for her own disinterest in marriage and family.

"I can't. I'm sorry——"

"You don't apologize, Christiana. This is going to be your day." She turned the young girl toward the mirror and eased the zipper down. "I have many more for you to consider."

"Thank god for that," her mother said in her most theatrical voice. "We're down to the wire. Three months. I don't know how this is going to get pulled off."

"Oh, you know your daughter has all the dressmakers from here to London willing to drop everything for her." Yvette drew back the train that cascaded down the three steps of the podium to help get it out of the way. "And for this beautiful bride."

Christiana smiled down at Yvette warmly. "Not if I pass out first. Oh, God, it feels good to be out of that." She took an exaggerated deep breath.

Her mother sighed deeply and returned to the long garment rack to seek out her version of wedding dress perfection.

"How about this one?" Claire pulled a puffy-sleeved gown reminiscent of Princess Diana's dress.

"It's fine." Christiana hadn't looked at the totally-wrong-for-her option, which was all Sarah needed to know. Something was very wrong. Perhaps Jonathan's instincts were dead on, which unnerved her.

"Mother, do you think you could find Madeline for me? She's in the back. Tell her I'll need the new shipment of Vera Wang's."

Her assistant would occupy them long enough for Sarah to get to the bottom of Christiana's mood.

"Oh, yes, a Vera Wang," her mother said. "There has to be something here. And, where are the other bridesmaids? I know I wouldn't miss this day given this is likely the only wedding I'm getting out of my children."

That last dig made just as her mother swiped back the curtain to the storeroom was for Sarah. Her only daughter failed to snag a wealthy husband by the time she was twenty-five, so in her mother's eyes, she was a dismal failure at womanhood.

Once she was sure her mother was out of earshot, she turned to Christiana. "What's wrong?"

"Nothing."

"Oh, really?"

"It's not polite to complain about your mother," Christiana offered. "But I swear we're going to elope before this is all over." She kicked the fabric at her feet.

"Easy there. That's a Mori Lee dress," Yvette said.

"Sorry. You're both being so nice and, well, do you know she wants to change the colors again? She says everyone is doing blue these days, and"—she adopted a snooty tone —"*God forbid that Marla Clampton wedding one-up you.* Like I could give a crap."

"I'll handle my mother. Don't you worry. What do *you* want?"

"I just want to be with Jonathan." She blinked with that wide-eyed innocence that had lured her step-brother as sure as sugar water did a hummingbird. Her guilelessness was no act. The young woman was no ingenue, either. She couldn't be and be involved with Jonathan—the man could be quite hardcore, especially in the bedroom. Yet somehow, she maintained a freshness, a vitality, that Sarah envied. She'd once had that feeling, where the world was new and offered so much she'd yet to experience. She could mark the day she'd lost her naivete around how the world worked. She shoved the memory back as she had for the last twenty years.

"I swear, Jonathan's being such a girl about the whole thing."

Yvette chuckled at how the young girl had hit that nail head with a sledgehammer.

"Don't tell him I said that," Christiana added quickly. "I know I shouldn't complain. He sacrificed a lot to be with me."

"Stop that." Sarah gripped Christiana's shoulders. "You love him. He loves you. There's no sacrifice in that. That's choosing. Now, dress shopping over. Go and find Jonathan. Talk to him. Tell him what's bothering you."

"I don't want to worry him."

"Trust me, he already is."

"Okay. Since I'm about to be super honest, you know what I want in a dress? Plain white silk—no frills, no blingy stuff. Something cut like this ..." She gestured around her hips and waist.

Sarah could see it—Christiana in nothing but one, perfectly cut silhouette with a gossamer veil a mile long, perhaps with tiny embedded crystals, the only embellishments and leaving a trail of sparkle behind her.

"I have just the thing." Sarah pulled out her cell phone, dialed Madeline in the back and told her assistant to hold all the Justin Alexander gowns they had. Something simple would drive her mother crazy—she who wanted enough fabric to cover the Capitol Building. However, the new dress would suit Christiana, and nothing would compete with her natural beauty. With that boost of energy, which always came after a styling conundrum had been handled, she turned to find the young girl stomping her foot into her practical black flats.

"Thanks, Sarah." Christiana threw her arms around her.

Sarah squeezed her back with no hesitation. It would take an ice queen not to accept the young girl's guileless warmth. Laurent was very similar to her, she mused.

"You'll tell your mother I had to go back to work?" Christiana asked.

"We've got this. You go on," Yvette answered.

After hugging Yvette good-bye, Christiana was out the door in a flash.

Sarah picked up an abandoned petticoat and began to gather the measuring tapes and pin cushions littering the tall pedestal before the three-way mirror.

"Don't worry, Sarah," Yvette said.

"Oh, I'm not."

"Oh, yes, you are. I can see it in your eyes. And you start to pace when things aren't sitting well with you."

Sarah took in her reflection. Good lord. She had concealer in her purse, didn't she? Those dark, under-eye circles matched her purple dress. "You're just seeing insomnia."

"Still?"

"Afraid so. Well, anyway, Christiana's just got cold feet. She's young."

"I can't imagine getting married at twenty-two. Oh, wait, I did, and see how that worked out. Divorced and scandalized."

"Ah, but we're talking Jonathan who will move the stars for her. Like your new love, Ryan will for you."

Yvette murmured at the sound of her second husband's name, and her eyes misted over as if in a far-off dream.

Sarah had witnessed the presence of true love many times, but it wasn't until this second that she realized how, one by one, the most important people in her life, all the Tribunal Council members, had committed to a whole new phase of their lives—first Jonathan with Christiana, then Yvette with Ryan.

Their mutual friend Carson had taken them all by surprise by falling harder than she thought possible for the equally formidable London. Then, another Council member, Mark, finally got his chance with Isabella, his brother's widow. However, the biggest surprise in the last few years was Derek. The resolute bachelor had finally met his match in Samantha, and they'd just welcomed their second child. Soon, from of the circle of her closest friends, she and Alexander would be the only single people left.

Her mother appeared behind her cradling a gown fit for a Quinceañera. "Where's Christiana?"

"Work," Yvette and Sarah said in unison.

"Work? Oh, for heaven's sake. That girl is going to be the death of me yet." Claire turned to return her armful of tulle and lace to the stockroom.

Yvette chuckled and ran her finger over a metal hanger that clanked in movement.

"So, tell me all about Steffan Vidar while helping me find a dress for tonight. His voice sounds handsome. Is he?" Yvette pulled out a hunter green dress that would make her look like death.

"That color will not do you justice, Yvette. Try this." Sarah pulled out a mint green cocktail dress with silver threads stitched at the neckline. She held it up. "Not bold, but no one else will be wearing it, and in a sea of DC black and blue, you'll stand out. To answer your question, yes, I'd describe Steffan as ... empirically quite handsome."

Her friend snatched the dress from her. "I knew you'd find me the perfect thing."

"Here, let me," Sarah saved Yvette's zipper by lowering it slowly.

"So, how do you know Steffan?" she asked.

"I met him at Club 501 in London two years ago." She'd stick with the facts for now.

"I love that club. So … classy medieval."

"Perfect description." Sarah laughed despite memories of all that red light sharpening the angles of Steffan's features making him appear like a marauding Viking—or what she thought one might look like.

"I understand Steffan has a delicious Spanish stud with him."

"Ah, so you've met Laurent Chacon." Just saying his name gave Sarah a jolt of positivity.

"No, I got a glance at him in the hallway outside Alexander's office before coming over today. Ryan filled me in on who he was." Yvette's eyes darted up to Sarah too quickly. "I heard he's with Steffan, but they aren't lovers. They're friends, so that means—"

"Wait, Laurent was alone?"

"No, he was with Carrie. They seemed quite friendly." Yvette turned to look at herself in the mirror. "Yes, this will do. And, you should wear red tonight. Steffan won't be able to take his eyes off you."

She laughed and waved her hand dismissively. People in love were always trying to get their friends to couple up.

She lowered her voice just in case her mother reappeared. "I'm sure Steffan merely wants to continue our conversation about his membership to Accendos. You know I vet the new members."

Yvette leaned closer. "Steffan sounds quite accomplished. I googled him. His water philanthropy has a 98% rating on Charity Navigator, has the backing of every major foundation in Europe, and rumor has it he's on track for a Nobel Prize."

Now that was a surprise. Then again, Steffan was full of

surprises, and she despised being caught off guard. "Well, good for him."

Yvette grasped her arm gently. "He sounds like quite a catch."

"I know where you're going, and please don't."

"You know I just want you to be happy, Sarah, and I sense …" Yvette chewed her lip.

"I'm fine, Yvette. Really."

"Well, what about a little harmless flirting?" She stepped up to the closest garment rack and pulled out the first red dress her hand landed on. "In this?"

It was the Theia red cocktail dress, and it was perfect. *Lucky pick.*

"When was the last time you drove a man to his knees?" she asked. "Wait, don't answer that; it was probably last night."

No, it had been a while. A mental image of a nude Laurent before her made her thighs tingle—and her mind spin with unwise ideas. Or, were they unwise? She did have a thought in the car ride over …

"Okay." She took the dress from her friend. "Call up Steffan. Tell him he has to bring Laurent. Then, put me next to him instead of Steffan, and I'll wear the red."

Yvette smiled. "Consider it done."

Sarah didn't often take advice, but her friendship with Yvette was not in competition with her dominance. Her friend was a hard-core submissive and making demands wasn't her modus operandi, but this mission would fulfill her hopeless romantic notions. If Steffan and Laurent were going to be at tonight's dinner, she wouldn't mind being a distraction for a certain male sub who'd offered himself to her. It also would put into place some order, starting with who was calling the shots.

As if divine timing, her mother swiped the curtain

between the main room and the storeroom. "Well, I'm off. Let me know when we're doing this again."

"We won't be," Sarah said. "You're off the hook, Mother. I have the dress for Christiana."

Her mother's face hardened for a second but then thawed when she caught Yvette watching her. "Well, then I guess there's nothing for me to do here."

"That's right. I've got it," Sarah said and smiled at herself in the mirror. Maybe she'd get her nails done in a matching red.

# 8

_____

The small private dining room of The Oak Room was ridiculously warm, and Steffan's patience had thinned in the oppressive air.

"Can't we just use desalinated ocean water?" The man took a large gulp of his drink.

"If you'd like to hurry our environmental and biological destruction, starting with turning off the Gulf Stream," Steffan said. "Within two decades, half of the world's population will be facing water shortages in one form or another. That includes the United States."

"Oh, it can't be that bad. We'll figure something out. The U.S. always does."

From the bored expression on the man's face, Steffan was having little impact on this man's conscience, but he never missed an opportunity to give the uninformed some sense of the approaching crisis.

He patted the man on the arm with a friendly smile. "Excuse me, I see someone I should speak to." Jonathan Brond had been eyeing him from his place before an unlit fireplace across the room for the last twenty minutes. Steffan held out his hand. "Jonathan."

The man pulled his hand from his pocket and met his handshake. "I see you're making the rounds, though I wouldn't count on Miles. He has money but no vision."

"Yes, I failed to convince him of much."

"There are plenty more deep pockets in this town. How is DC treating you otherwise?"

"Everyone has been quite welcoming."

"And Laurent? He settling in?" Jonathan inclined his head toward Laurent who was chatting with two young girls. Steffan chuckled at their coquettish hair touching and head-tilting actions. Laurent had that effect on both genders, but the men admirers were subtler.

"Let me introduce you to him" Steffan raised his hand, catching Laurent's eye. Laurent nodded and extricated himself gracefully from the two girls.

"How long are you in town?" Jonathan swirled the ice in his glass.

"At least a year." He met the man's eyes directly, knowing he was being assessed—had been since he and Laurent had walked in.

"Ah, Laurent. I want you to meet someone. Jonathan Brond, this is my dear friend, Laurent Chacon, Jonathan is one of Alexander's friends and Sarah's brother."

"A pleasure, sir."

Laurent and Jonathan exchanged hearty handshakes, and then Laurent lowered his gaze. Most vanilla people wouldn't catch his friend's subtle, automatic reaction when surrounded by established dominance. By the smug appreciation filling his eyes, Jonathan had.

"Laurent, do you mind?" Steffan handed him his empty glass.

Laurent immediately took the tumbler from his fingers and spun on his heel.

"I didn't realize Laurent was your slave," Jonathan said.

"He's not. He enjoys being useful."

At a slap on his shoulder, he turned to find Derek had joined them. "Steffan, you've got no drink, man. You won't last long here sober."

"It's coming. Good to see you again, Derek."

"I understand you two have met," Jonathan said.

"Yes. The Dragon Club in Copenhagen. Amazing place." Derek waggled his eyebrows.

"Not as amazing as Alexander's," Steffan noted.

A quick glance around showed no one had paid much attention to them, but he found it curious that Derek and Jonathan would say anything at all about their mutual recreation in vanilla company.

"You're right there. You should come by Frost, my new club. Not much to do there but drink and dance and admire gorgeous women, but sometimes that's all that's needed."

"You'd be right at home," a loud male voice said behind him. "Frost is Scandinavian-themed. Ryan Knightbridge, Yvette's other half." The large man thrust out his hand, which Steffan took. He recognized Ryan from his initial tour of Accendos, where Ryan had a particularly sultry brunette, whom he now knew was Yvette, tied to a spanking bench in The Library.

"Laurent and I will have to stop by," Steffan said.

"I hear you like the club scene. Been to quite a few?" Jonathan asked. Ryan and Derek held his gaze as if the answer to that question was going to be the most interesting thing they heard that night.

"Well, as often as time permits." He no longer had any doubts about tonight's real purpose. They wanted to see how he handled himself in public. He wondered how many other

Accendos members attended tonight given the presence of half the governing Tribunal. So long as their judgements didn't hinder his and Laurent's ability to join Accendos, he didn't care what conclusions they drew.

A flash of red in the doorway caught his attention and Jonathan's face softened. *Sarah.* She had paused and casually scanned from one end of the room to the other as if she hadn't made up her mind which way to head. Her eyes landed on Laurent, and she strode toward him, drink in hand. Even from this distance, Steffan could see her reaction to Laurent. The slight lift of her lips, the tenderness filling her eyes were all signs that Laurent's effect on her was the same as most people he encountered. *Captivated.* She also had a similar, bewitching effect on people, albeit for different reasons. Her power caused people to straighten in their seats. Laurent's made them melt their pants. What a combination they would be.

A soft chime rang, announcing dinner was about to be served, which shook his reverie.

"Well, if you'll excuse me, gentleman, I'm afraid I can't stay for dinner. I have to meet my fiancé." Jonathan placed his empty glass on the mantle and strode toward Sarah, ending Steffan's plan to intercept her before dinner started.

## 9

"Where's Christiana?" Sarah presented her cheek to Jonathan for the obligatory DC peck.

"Working. I'm picking her up soon. I wanted to thank you again for handling her wedding dress and our earlier chat."

"Helping her is a joy to me, and, when it comes to my mother, Christiana should become unreachable. It's what I do."

"Her new job means her cell phone is within arm's length at all times."

"Consider what I said. Elope."

"You may be the only person on earth who can tell me what to do." He chuckled softly.

"Because you know I'm right?"

"Because I know you have my best interests at heart. Give my love to Yvette. I'm not staying for dinner." He glanced toward Steffan who cleaved a path through the dining room. Jonathan leaned down to her. "He can't take his eyes off you."

She rolled her eyes at him and watched his broad back disappear through the doorway. When she turned, she came face-to-face with Steffan wearing yet another expensively-cut, blue suit. "May I escort you to your seat?"

"You may."

"You didn't return my call."

"I've been busy. It seems you have been, as well."

Steffan led her to her seat, sandwiched between Laurent on her right and an old friend, Michael Standish on her left. He pulled out her chair and leaned down to her ear. "Would you have returned a call two years ago?"

"We will never know, will we?" She scooted her own chair in. "Hello, Michael."

Steffan chuckled lightly. She lost Michael's greeting, distracted by the feeling of Steffan's breath in her hair.

Laurent slipped into the seat on her other side, and she turned to him.

"It's good to see you, Laurent."

"You, as well."

"I trust you haven't found DC too boring over the last few days?"

"With the amount of renovation required for one newly-acquired townhouse, I don't think 'bored' is going to be possible," he said and glanced at Steffan, who elegantly folded his tall frame into the too-tight space across the table from her—another signature move of Yvette ensuring shoulder-to-shoulder intimacy. That navy fabric certainly brought out his blue eyes, something he probably knew and planned.

"Alexander has quite an interest in home renovations," she said. "He'd be delighted to counsel you."

"Oh, I wouldn't dream of bothering Ma—Mr. Rockingham." Had Laurent caught himself from saying Master? That moniker definitely would have piqued curiosity here.

"Have you met Alexander yet?"

"Not formally. I would love to be introduced to him—I think," he added with a laughing frown.

She understood his hesitation. Many submissives found Alexander awe-inspiring.

"I have lunch with him tomorrow," Steffan interjected, snapping his napkin into place.

"Bring your appetite. Alexander enjoys large lunches."

"My appetite has never been a problem." He brought his wine glass to his lips, those deep blue eyes nailed on hers.

"Well, I understand we're having surf and turf tonight," Michael said.

"Something for everyone," Sarah said.

"Except Laurent," Steffan said.

"Vegetarian?"

"No, just particular …" Steffan answered for him.

"Steffan is a great cook," Laurent explained. "Do you like Italian? He makes his own pasta. I think you'd enjoy it."

"And what do you enjoy, Laurent?"

He leaned closer to her. "I'd enjoy you." His voice was too soft to be heard by Michael who'd moved on to the woman to his left.

"Flirt." She laughed.

When Laurent cast his eyes downward, a half smile formed on her lips. A blush of pink traveled up his beautiful neck. *So sweet.* Perhaps Yvette was right. A little harmless teasing never hurt anyone, and his attentions were so … warming.

"I heard you're trying to raise funds for digging wells in developing countries." Mrs. Darden sat on Steffan's left and by the size of her cat-like smile was quite happy with the seating arrangement. She always liked to be in the know when new people came to town.

"Yes, that's one project," he said. "And Laurent is getting his degree in physical therapy."

"Good heavens. You'll have to *touch* people, dear." She brought a hand to her breast, aghast as she looked at Laurent.

"That's what I hear," Laurent murmured.

"You'll help a great number of people, Laurent." Sarah winked at him and gazed across the table at Steffan. "Mr. Vidar, on the other hand, is all about energy and water." She had done her research before she'd arrived. "Seems the next war on this planet is going to be access to clean water. Not enough to go around, isn't that right?"

He lifted his glass once more and squinted at her. "You'd be amazed at how many people don't have their basic needs met."

"I would, and one should always start with the basic needs of people."

"Oh, my, are we onto solving the world's problems already?" Mrs. Darden laughed.

A large man's shoe touched hers. Steffan's? She pulled her feet further underneath her seat.

"Not all the world's problems," Steffan said.

That *was* his foot that had slipped in-between hers.

"Just the most pressing ones." He had the nerve to smile.

"But then, not everything is as pressing as one makes it out to be." She pulled her feet back so he'd have to slouch to reach her.

Laurent signaled at the waiter walking by with a water pitcher and pointed to Sarah's empty water goblet. The man stopped and refilled Sarah's glass.

"Tell me, Miss Marillioux, what do you find to be the most pressing issues of the day?" Steffan asked.

"Oh, God, please don't tell me we're going to talk politics now," Mrs. Darden groaned. "All that struggle for power. It's so tedious."

"I couldn't agree with you more, Mrs. Darden," returned Sarah.

"Really?" Steffan asked. "I thought the women's movement right now was all about righting the imbalance of power."

She shrugged. "I have never believed I *didn't* have power."

"Good," Steffan said. "Powerful women turn me on."

Mrs. Darden's eyes snapped to him, though he pretended not to notice.

Laurent interrupted, perhaps uncomfortable at the verbal jousting between her and Steffan? She, on the other hand, was rather warming up to it. "Would you like some wine?" he asked.

"No, thank you," she said.

Steffan's eyes pierced her from across the table. "I appreciate women who own their power—whether that be to share it or wield it. Laurent, what about you?"

"Me? I like all women," he said without a hitch and raised his water glass. Mrs. Darden nodded in his direction and smiled.

"How diplomatic of you, Laurent," Sarah said. "I believe Steffan wanted to know how dominant you like your partners." She arched an eyebrow at Steffan in question.

She could play this little secret game he'd started to play. It sure beat talking about politics, and the look on Mrs. Darden's face was worth letting her irritation at the smug Swede go.

"Yes, Miss Marillioux, you are quite correct."

She turned to Laurent. "Well, Laurent, what do you like?"

"I like a strong partner," he said, meeting her gaze so ardently she felt as if his eyes had kissed her face.

She glanced down at his lap—and his erection punching at his pants. A pang hit her in her core, and then damn, if Steffan's foot wasn't between hers again. When was the last time a man touched her without explicit permission? Years? Two years ago, to be exact.

"I like my men strong, too. In all kinds of ways." She

leaned toward Laurent and whispered in his ear. "Especially those who are unafraid to please."

The apple of his cheek rose with his smile and brushed across her skin. The raze of his slight five o'clock shadow scraped her skin and sent tingles up her neck. The room had grown warm, and Laurent's scent—a mix of expensive summer wool and an unnamed spicy men's cologne—drifted in the air. Without looking at Steffan, she eased her feet back, dragging her heels along the side of his foot. Despite his earlier jokes about her "death heels," she knew their effect on him. He'd asked her to keep them on *that night.* She had—for a while—until they moved to the shower.

Over the years, she'd purposefully dulled the details of that night in her mind, the deep blue of his eyes, his scent, his criminally perfect body—one designed to pull off a tightly tailored suit like the one he wore. All were details she'd shoveled into some mental compartment she'd refused to open. Tonight, a shock of blond hair kept falling into his eyes and … Jesus, she was admiring the man. This wouldn't do. His suitability to join the Accendos family had to be formulated on facts, not feelings.

"Tell me about your house renovations," she said to Laurent and laid her hand gently on his leg for a long moment.

Red once more colored his neck, but god love him, he began to speak about quartz countertops and specially-ordered bathroom fixtures. They were cold things that called up the practicalities of life, in other words, nothing romantic.

As the four-course dinner unfolded, she divided her time between small talk with Michael and learning more about Laurent's role as "house manager," as he dubbed himself. Thankfully, Steffan's attentions were taken up by Mrs. Darden who, after overhearing Laurent's remarks about home renovations, kept him quite occupied with recommendations on contractors in Washington DC.

Laurent did not drink a drop of alcohol during dinner. She also abstained because an idea formed halfway through the main course.

She dabbed her napkin on her lips. "Well, gentleman, it's been a wonderful evening. Laurent, would you see me home?" She spoke loudly. If others overheard, Steffan would be less inclined to balk at her request, as if he had the right to anyway.

"I'd be delighted." Laurent rose and reached for her chair.

She felt every bit of Steffan's amused face as she lifted herself from her seat.

He unfolded himself, taking Mrs. Darden's hand with him. He kissed it, causing a rare blush from the woman, his move rendering her speechless. He looked back at Sarah. "Laurent and I drove here. I'd hate to have him dependent on Uber or a taxi. We'll both see you home. Two is always better than·one."

*We'll see.*

After they said their good-byes to Yvette and a few others, Sarah found Laurent at the entrance, her spring wrap held out in an offering.

"Why thank you, Laurent."

Steffan held the door open for them both, and they slipped out into the chilly spring air.

"Really, Steffan, you don't need—"

"Oh, yes, I do." He handed his valet ticket to the attendant. "Then tomorrow, we will continue our discussions ... all three of us together?"

"Why wait?" she asked. "Alexander's is always open. We'll go now." Good, surprise on his face was what she was going for. When she'd said "home" she hadn't said exactly which one, and playing this early in the vetting process, provided it included a Council member, wasn't forbidden. It was within her power to choose if and when.

"Excellent," he said. "I had hoped we might pick up where we'd left off in London."

Now that her car was pulling up, she stepped off the curb. When she'd slipped out to the ladies' room earlier, she'd asked the valet staff to make sure her car arrived precisely at 8:30. "I have something else in mind. Follow me."

# 10

Tony, Alexander's most trusted bodyguard, stood at the top of the step when she pulled up to Accendos' main entrance.

"Good evening, Tony," she said and gave him her keys. "I'm bringing in Steffan Vidar and Laurent Chacon. I'll take it from here."

"Mr. Rockingham asked me to come down and see if you needed anything."

"Alexander?" *Of course.* On the ride over, Sarah had called Carrie and instructed her on what to prepare. Carrie would have filled Alexander in, anticipating he likely wanted to be the person who could witness the new participant's consent to play. The man also had a knack for anticipating her plans, like suddenly bringing Steffan and Laurent to the club.

She was pleased to see the two men pull in behind her car and within seconds join her at the entrance. Tony opened the door for them.

"Tony, will you see Laurent to The Library? I need a word with Steffan. That's all right with you, Laurent, isn't it?" She turned to Laurent.

"Of course. I'll leave you both to it." Was that a smirk she saw on Laurent's face as he slipped by and followed Tony out? For a submissive, she rather liked that he showed these off-character moments. He moved from acquiescence to opinionated male so quickly, it made her hands itch to grasp his cheeks and tell him exactly how she treated petulance—even the endearing kind.

As soon as she and Steffan were alone in the portico, she circled the large round table, tuning into the sweet scent of the white French tulips that spilled gracefully from a large glass bowl. Her thoughts came together better when she was moving.

"You needn't be nervous," Steffan said.

"I'm not."

"You pace whenever we're about to address unfamiliar territory."

He'd been studying her movements? She stopped in front of him. "I'd like to play alone with Laurent. You can observe. And, before you say no, you've had three glasses of wine, which is one more than Accendos allows in a twenty-four hour period for playtime."

He scratched his five o'clock shadow. "Another time then?"

"Worried I don't know what I'm doing? May I remind you, you two approached me?"

"Fair enough. But there are things you need to know."

"So tell me."

"You know his limits, I presume?"

"I am familiar with the list you sent over, yes." She'd memorized the rather short list—too short in her estimation. "Tell me what's not on there." If she'd learned anything over the years, submissives were never to be trusted to reveal everything.

"When it comes to playing alone with a Mistress, he

enjoys being taken to the edge again and again. Don't let him come."

"Why not?"

"You know you could ask him all these things directly. I don't own him."

"Yet you protect him."

"Sometimes from himself. In fact, I challenged him not to come all week."

"Is that how you two operate?"

"I'm not his Master, but when he's without someone, I offer a certain level of discipline. It's not enough for him long-term, but he needs to be useful and for him, following rules—like those I laid out—is vital to his well-being, his confidence."

"Creative."

"Necessary. Service and structure are in his blood."

"What if he fails a task or breaks a rule?"

"He doesn't. And if he succeeds, we share someone —together."

Her lips parted. "Interesting reward."

"Works for me." His eyes colored with that signature arrogance. "So you see, we both have a vested interest in him succeeding."

"Perhaps another time, Steffan," she said with a smile. Like she'd let him touch her again tonight? *Bad boy.* And, with that thought, desire snaked up her inner thighs to her core and smoldered. She did her best to smother it.

He lifted his chin and looked down at her. "Tell you what, if you wish for him to come undone, I will allow it. One time. *Only one.* His refraction period is staggeringly short. You'll have to watch that."

"Laurent is capable of multiple orgasms in one evening?" Steffan nodded. Her eyebrow raised in curiosity and antici- pation. *How delicious.*

"If he climaxes more than once, then you and I must agree on the punishment," Steffan added.

"Agreed." She was, after all, shutting Steffan out, and he and Laurent had a long-term, if unusual, relationship. She took a deep breath. "Anything else?"

"Don't be surprised if you fall in love. Immediately."

"I don't fall in love—ever," Sarah scoffed.

"Never? How boring."

"How wise." She headed down the hall to a waiting Laurent. Steffan prowled several steps behind.

With every foot drawn closer to The Library, she willed herself to more calmness. She needed to have her whole head in what they were about to do. Her self-control must be absolute.

Inside, Carrie waited for her, standing next to Alexander. Laurent knelt at their feet wearing nothing but those Slimane Dior Homme trousers that hugged his hips and ass so perfectly. He'd already stripped his shirt, shoes, and socks. She'd address that independent decision with him later. She enjoyed both dressing and undressing men.

When Sarah stopped in front of him, he lowered his forehead to the ground. His immediate generosity warmed her heart, and that familiar jolt of power moved up her legs.

"Laurent, look at me."

He lifted his head.

"Are you sure you wish to be here?" she asked.

"Yes, Mistress Sarah. I asked to be here. I crave it, actually." The beautiful man peered up at her with those dark gypsy eyes that could so easily undo her self-discipline. He was going to test her as much as she would him.

"Very good," Alexander said. "Consent granted." He smiled at her warmly before heading out the door.

"What was that about?" Steffan asked.

"Anyone who plays for the first time at Accendos must

have their consent witnessed by a third party, someone not connected to the scene directly."

"So many rules."

"You have no idea," Carrie said. "Oh, sorry, Mistress Sarah. Master Steffan."

"That'll be all, Carrie." Sarah turned to Steffan. "Rules are what make us who we are."

"I rather believed our characters were made up of more than that."

She turned away from the man who looked entirely too self-satisfied for being shut out of a scene. He lowered himself to the large, dark green velvet chair usually reserved for Alexander. Steffan fit the large chair, and Carrie knelt near him. So she found him intriguing, as well? She couldn't blame the girl. Steffan was a living, Better Business Bureau advertisement for Sweden—all Viking blond good looks and ice blue eyes, and Carrie was single.

Sarah turned to what the girl had prepared for her. A large wooden chest on canisters sat a few feet away, and even before cracking it open, she was confident Carrie had filled it with every item she'd requested. She rolled the goodies to where Laurent knelt.

She crouched down to him and cupped his chin. She scrutinized his eyes, now reflecting the red and orange colors of the recessed lighting in The Library.

"Do you enjoy being watched, Laurent?"

"It doesn't matter. I won't notice anyone but you."

"Such lovely words."

"Truth."

"Which are the only words I want to hear from you." She released his chin and placed her palm against his heart, feeling the pulse of blood underneath that smooth skin. A slight dusting of hair was rough under her hand. She appreciated aesthetics more than most—made a career out of it—

but nothing, *nothing*, compared to the natural beauty of his tan skin. She had a strong impulse to scrape her nails down his chest, and as she raked down his sternum to his belly, she left red welts on his skin. The marks faded in seconds.

"I'll stop if I think you're not being honest," she said.

"Yes, Mistress." His chest rose and fell in a deep breath, but his voice hadn't wavered a bit.

She stood and spent a long moment assessing the man kneeling at her feet.

On the way to Accendos, she'd given some thought to how she'd like to approach Laurent this first time. Sensory deprivation with some CBT would be the obvious choice. According to his records, his favorite type of play was having his cock and balls tortured. He liked to watch his Dom or Domme handle him, too, which meant only one thing. She'd blindfold him.

She cracked open the top of the chest, and two drawers lifted and separated to either side. She chose a black cotton blindfold along with a pair of thick leather cuffs. Laurent's eyes glanced up and grew wide when she showed him what she held.

"Something wrong, Laurent?"

He shook his head and lowered his chin.

"Take off your trousers and your briefs. Fold them. Let Steffan hold them." She winked at Steffan who smirked at her words, not looking the least bit bothered by being reduced to the role of valet.

Laurent complied, giving her a spectacular view of his backside when he strode over to Steffan. When he turned to her, she decided his front rivaled his back. Glossy, dark curls surrounded a long, thick cock that had already begun to harden. With the dusting of dark hair across his chest, visible ridges in his abdomen and a perfectly-defined Adonis belt, his masculine appeal grew tenfold. He could have modeled for the Greek masters, though they might be appalled at the size of his spectacular sexual anatomy.

"So beautiful, Laurent," she whispered.

He flushed. Another honest moment that told her what she suspected—the man had no idea how beautiful he was.

She led him to the exact spot where she'd literally dreamed of taking him—a large frame in the center of the room from which various hooks and chains hung. She encircled his neck with the blindfold and let the fabric hang and tease his mind with the promise of coming blindness. The cotton was light, but she sensed he'd feel it like a lead chain. She fastened a cuff around each of his thick wrists.

"Lift your arms over your head."

She stepped up on one of the frame's rungs and attached each cuffed wrist to a hook that hung from chains. She stepped down and took a long moment to run her hands down his forearms to his biceps, and then over his shoulders. She never trussed her submissives too tightly, preferring to see them move and sway as she worked them over—unless they required a more bound approach. She'd learn Laurent's preferences and dole them out either as rewards or punishments over time.

He sucked in a breath when she pinched a nipple. "Laurent. I'm glad you're here."

He returned her stare with no hesitation. "Wherever, whenever you need me."

The pretty words tumbled from his mouth with such ease, her knees weakened. His eyes sparked with desire, his breath running a little faster across those full lips. A submissive's reactions could be a performance, a make-believe arousal meant to incite a Dom or Domme's courage. She knew *his* response was genuine, and her sense of obligation to him heightened because of it.

She took more minutes to appreciate his flesh with her

hands. God, she wanted to test every inch of that skin—feel, taste, and mark it. She'd wanted to play with Laurent the first day she'd laid eyes on him, which was dangerous. Her past led her to distrust desire, and that caution had paid dividends. Yet, there was much to explore with a man this transparent—the direct opposite of his current Dominant sitting in Alexander's chair.

"I loved your file, Laurent. Loved reading about you. What you enjoy, what you don't. I can't wait to test some of those limits." She showed him the ball stretcher and cock ring apparatus. "I understand your cock requires a Mistress's discipline."

One glance south and she realized she'd chosen well. He thickened further, which sent his cock dancing. That was the thing about male anatomy, unlike their mouths, their manhood never lied.

She smiled up at him. "It pleases me to see your responses. Don't hold anything back, Laurent. Do you understand?"

"Yes, Mistress."

"Safeword?"

"I won't use it."

"Speak it out loud for me."

"Polyester."

She laughed. "Oh, you already please me, you wonderful man."

He gave her a flash of white teeth against that smooth tanned skin.

She then gently curled her fingers around his cock and forgot everything else—even Steffan.

## 11

Steffan studied Sarah's elegant hands as she affixed the ring around Laurent's ample girth and pulled his balls through the stretcher. She stepped back to admire her work. She cocked her hip and the red fabric of her dress stretched tight across her behind. Was there anything so mesmerizing as a woman's ass? A long line of muscle ran up her thigh. She carried the hint of a dimple in her butt cheek like a thoroughbred horse. He couldn't take his eyes off her shape and her skin, especially that bare, smooth flesh of her leg. God, he wanted to force them open and direct her to wrap them around his waist while he buried himself in her.

Sarah tsked and his attention moved to Laurent. Steffan had been so entranced by the woman, he'd missed what Laurent had done—or not done—to earn a strike across his backside. Laurent grunted and smiled as Sarah continued to appreciate him with her hands. She circled him, ran her fingers across Laurent's pecs, trailed light touches around his shoulders, and up and down his back.

"You have no idea how magnificent you look like this, do you, my sweet man?" she whispered.

No, Laurent didn't comprehend his effect on others. His natural good looks were called up from another world. Instead, he was outwardly fixated. He never thought of himself, another reason Steffan feared leaving the man in anyone's hands but his own—or Sarah's whom he oddly trusted as he did no other. He didn't trust Alexander Rockingham, whose rules and regulations meant to protect both submissive and Dominant alike were famous, as much as he trusted Sarah.

Laurent shuddered under her light touch, and his chest began to rise and fall.

She pressed her breasts into his back, her fingers finding their way around his abdomen to that cock cage. She seemed to be assuring herself it was staying on. Steffan knew better. She teased Laurent whose hardness now strained inside its cage, precum wetting the tip. The angle of Steffan's chair gave him quite a view of it.

"Hmm, next time I might have to get a larger ring," she said into Laurent's ear.

"I'm fine, Mistress."

"Your cock needs something tight? It's that undisciplined?" She slapped his ass cheek, and he pitched forward in his cuffs.

"Perhaps a spiked ring," she said into his shoulder blade and bit down. Laurent groaned. The man appreciated rough play, which she'd learn soon enough.

She rubbed her breasts up and down his back, and Laurent's mouth opened. Steffan felt his cock stiffen in response to her movements. He didn't have a submissive inclination in his body, but he wouldn't mind being on the receiving end of those undulations. He knew what she felt like as she arched her back—as she did now against Laurent.

She slipped the blindfold over his eyes. Laurent did what he always did when a sense was taken away, he stiffened and strained, his fingers curling into fists. The loss of sight terrified him, which is why Steffan had been introducing it more and more. He didn't want Laurent to be frightened of anything. Interesting, how Sarah chose to introduce that from the get-go.

"I'm right here, Laurent," she said.

"Y-yes Mistress."

"You can do this for me, can't you?"

He nodded. She hadn't done anything of note to him yet, but Steffan admired her ability to ratchet up Laurent's imagination with what she might do in such few words—and her kindness to check in with him so soon into their play.

"I'm going to warm you up a little." She tweaked his nipple between her thumb and index finger.

"Thank you, Mistress," he grunted out.

"Carrie, bring it to me."

Carrie jumped up and retrieved a riding crop from an umbrella stand he hadn't noticed had been placed next to the wooden chest. Interesting that Sarah chose that instrument. He'd have gone with something stronger. Then again, she'd only begun, and she'd soon learn how much Laurent could take—how much he *wanted* to take.

She ran the leather tongue of the crop over Laurent's pecs. "Such splendid nipples, Laurent."

She opened her palm and Carrie placed two ordinary clothespins in her hand. Laurent cried out as Sarah snapped them on. He stomped a foot and breathed heavily through clenched teeth.

"Those are ordinary wooden clothespins, Laurent. You'll have to earn something nicer."

"Nice choice, Sarah," Steffan muttered under his breath. Laurent loved clothes, preened in 18-carat gold cufflinks and often enjoyed sporting an old-fashioned pocket watch connected to a sterling silver chain in his vest pocket. Ordinary clothes pins would be somewhat humiliating, as Laurent would have expected something in pure silver given the opulence of this club. It was then Steffan realized she could be cruel as well as kind. Laurent was going to be in heaven.

"I didn't hear a thank you, Mistress," she said.

"Sorry, Mistress. Thank you, Mistress," he panted.

She tapped one of the clothespins, and he sucked in a breath between his teeth. She glanced at Carrie who knelt by the small chest and smiled as if they shared a secret. So, Sarah liked an audience. Steffan enjoyed being part of that, watching Sarah, admiring her. He would enjoy being part of her scene more, though she made herself clear by shutting him out. He'd allow her this moment of respite because seeing her like this again … He gripped the sides of the chair and made a decision. Tonight, she'd have Laurent to herself. Any other night? It would be both of them.

# 12

Some people believe a riding crop is child's play. An instrument used in movies and in books whenever BDSM is portrayed. How wrong people can be. If used properly, over a long period of time, that tiny leather square, slapping flesh, could bring the most hardened submissive to heel.

Sarah ran the leather tongue over his shoulders, down his spine to rest at the cleft of his ass. She pushed the long handle through his cheeks, and then up and under his testicles. She pressed against his back and held it there.

"So hard for me." She jerked the crop upward feeling it press into the separation of his two balls. He inhaled sharply.

"What am I going to do with you?" she asked.

She didn't need to be in front of him to know he'd swallowed in honest anticipation.

She then went to work on his back and thighs. Light slaps followed by harder ones, never letting a rhythm form to keep him on edge, keep him guessing. A harlequin pattern bloomed on his back and his thighs. She'd purposefully avoided slapping him on his ass, and he'd begun, either consciously or unconsciously, to pitch backward like he was seeking contact. So, she studiously avoided that area. Oh, yes, cruel and kind was such a dance.

"Mistress? Please?" he asked.

"Please what, my impatient boy?"

Steffan said he'd enjoyed being taken to the edge. She could do that. She turned him to face the other way so quickly he stumbled on his feet, but he easily righted himself with her help.

"Present that undisciplined cock to me, Laurent."

He rocked his torso up and forward with such eagerness, she could have grown enthralled by the sight of him. His abdomen muscles tensed, the ridges more pronounced, the dusting of hair trailing down in a V glistening under the lights. She ran a fingertip down each deep crevice of his Adonis belt.

"My second favorite part of a man," she whispered.

"What's your favorite?" Steffan's voice cut through her appreciation. It was rude of him to interrupt this moment, so she ignored him.

Her fingers made their way down to his captured cock and balls. She ran feather-light touches over its satin skin, knowing the sensation would be tripled given its captivity and engorgement. Time to show more gratitude for his gift to her.

She stepped back, breaking all contact, and his body tried to follow. She tapped the underside of his scrotum with the crop, once, twice, three times and then fell into a rhythm, the first of the night, moving across every inch of his captured hardness.

"Such a beautiful red, Laurent." The skin stretched taut over his balls was tight and bright crimson. She popped the leather tongue on them once more. He cried out a little.

"You can go five more minutes, can't you?"

"Y-yes, mistress."

She struck him on his cock, over and over, the slap-grunt-slap-grunt turning into its own rhythm. He strained in his bonds, and a tear dripped down his cheek on her last strike.

She cupped his jaw and slipped the blindfold down. He wiped sweat from his forehead along his bicep and blinked at the sudden invasion of light. His eyelashes had grown spiky with wet, and his eyes shone a fierce longing. Desire thrummed through her body. She widened her stance as she fell into his brown eyes for a long moment. Was there anything so invigorating to one's soul, to one's sense of existence, than to be connected to another like this?

It had been a long time since she'd played, and here she had one of the most beautiful males she'd ever laid eyes on swaying in front of her. He'd come to her, asked for her, lured her to him, and then he'd laid himself before her to do as she wished. She sucked in a long breath to steady herself. One could grow too heady with such a thought. *He's a gift. Remember, a temporary gift.*

She moved to her next instrument, a flogger with long tails that had clusters of leather roses at the end. One could mistake them for being merely aesthetic given their elegance and soft elk's hide material. They'd be wrong. The soft thumps they made belied the effect of their impact, and soon Laurent's grunts, a deep baritone at first, moved to something more high-pitched, as she circled him, landing blows on shoulders, back, and thighs.

She pointed to the evil stick, and Carrie retrieved it. She snapped it across Laurent's ass, once, twice, three times. A stream of tears ran down his cheek at the last strike, his cry a vulgar curse. The cords in his neck were so pronounced she was worried they might snap, and the head of his cock had turned a vicious purple.

"Laurent," she asked in his ear. "Where are you? Number?"

"Eight," A wet hiss through clenched teeth that held anger and pain.

"Ah."

"Just the way I like it," he breathed. "More."

"No."

Her desire competed with her common sense, but the latter won. He wanted more play, but he was going to get something better from her tonight—her full responsibility.

She focused on his pleading eyes. "Breathe," she instructed and then walked behind him.

He took in a stuttered breath.

She pressed herself into Laurent's back, sweat and musk seeping into her clothes, her skin. She ran her hands up his taut arm muscles but couldn't reach the cuffs, and she didn't want to break contact with him. "Steffan, will you?"

Steffan rocketed out of his chair. She'd expected him to stand in from of Laurent and help her lower him, but instead, he pressed against her, his hard-on like a steel bar against her back, and flattened her into Laurent.

She let out a hiss as she turned her head. Being taken by surprise this way was unconscionable. She wasn't the sub here, damn-it.

His hands mirrored her own movements, running up her arms to her wrists and then to the clips that held Laurent in place. He unhooked them and lowered Laurent's arms down slowly to his front. The three of them stood there, swaying, held up mostly by Steffan—the bastard. She had invited him to help, but not this way, this intimate sandwiching of her between them.

"Laurent, grab the chains," she said.

Steffan never let go of the man's wrists. He raised them again so Laurent could curl his fists around the links. Steffan pivoted on one foot and was in front of Laurent immediately. Laurent collapsed in his arms. It pissed her off, his ability to carry Laurent when her petite frame wouldn't allow it. But then, that had always been the case. She'd always had help lowering a male larger than her—which was most of them. It was her own damned fault for choosing the center of the room without a frame or furniture to help ease him down. She willed back a rise of anger.

"Here," she pointed to the soft floor mat in front of the hanging chains. "Put him here."

Steffan did what she asked. She knelt, sitting on one hip and cradled Laurent's head in her hands. She raked her fingernails slowly over his slick chest. "Breathe, my sweet man."

He gave her a lazy smile.

"Carrie, bring me that pillow?" After placing it under his head, she went to work checking his cock and balls. She undid the straps and slowly released the pressure. Laurent hissed as the blood redistributed itself.

He looked up into her eyes. "Magic," he whispered.

She pushed damp hair off his face and smiled down at him. "Just fly." By the way his eyes had dilated, the man was in orbit.

"Come with me."

"Oh, I am." And, she was. Despite Steffan's interruption, she hadn't such energy course through her in a while. "You are …" She couldn't finish her words. What was he? Magnificent? Beautiful? Wonderful? All the things Doms say to their submissives. Something about Laurent was so different, however. He was pure. Steffan was right. Anyone would be challenged not to fall in love with this man. She, however, would keep all feelings where they belonged—contained—for the safety of both of them. Laurent had earned it, and she wouldn't betray his trust with anything but perfection.

## 13

Steffan eased Laurent down into the large king-sized bed. Sarah had insisted on her private bedroom for aftercare. He'd known all the Tribunal Council members had private rooms for their use at Accendos. The size of the room and the king-sized bed, however, was quite the surprise. Alexander's home had originally been designed at the turn of the century. Clearly, the man had done extensive renovations, as her room not only boasted a bay window overlooking the gardens, but all the conveniences of modern-day life including a private bathroom with large Jacuzzi tub and separate shower, lined in marine blue, glass tiles. He noticed the spa-like opulence through the open doorway.

Carrie set a washcloth on Laurent's forehead, straightened and looked over at Sarah who appeared still high from the scene.

"Thank you, Carrie," Sarah said. "That's all for now. It's late, why don't you go home?"

The young girl simply nodded and slipped out the door.

"Carrie's quite good for someone so young." Steffan

pulled the covers up around Laurent's shoulders. "Laurent often chills after a hard scene."

"She's lived a longer life than you can imagine. Ex-cop from Boston."

He straightened. "Then someone's been putting something in the water. Everyone appears younger than they are here at Accendos."

"Happiness is the fountain of youth. Let's talk out in the hall. Let Laurent sleep. He can stay here tonight."

"No, I'll take him home. He'll crash hard if he wakes in unfamiliar surroundings."

"I see. As you wish." She glanced at Laurent one last time before heading toward the door. He recognized that look in her eyes—longing. He'd once put that in her eyes for him.

Steffan followed her out, admiring the way her hips elegantly swayed if such a thing was possible.

"Is that your secret then?" he asked, closing the door softly behind them.

"What do you mean?"

"You're so agelessly beautiful because you are happy?"

She chuckled softly. "Very good, Steffan. Two compliments in one."

"Not a compliment. The truth."

"Well, I was just gifted something wonderful by that man lying in my bed." She focused on the bedroom door as if she could see Laurent on the other side. Though clearly she was still flying, her eyes dropped a little, and her shoulders pitched slightly forward. She was tired.

He reached out and moved a lock of her hair over her ear.

She didn't balk at his move, a good sign.

"Laurent enjoys your handling," Steffan said. "And you enjoy him."

"I do."

"You didn't have him come."

"Perhaps next time. You said he liked being taken to the edge."

"So, you'll want to take things further now?"

"We'll see."

"Don't play with him, Sarah."

"Isn't that why you're here. To *play*." Her sudden irritation caught him off guard.

"You know what I mean."

She crossed her arms. "No. Why don't you say exactly what you mean?"

"Don't take him heaven and then drop him off in hell. Don't. Fuck. Him. Over." He scrubbed his hair. "I ... apologize. You wouldn't do that. I'm ..." He looked away, mastered his anger. "I'm not good at watching." "

"Thank you."

And, didn't that irk him, how she thanked him for apologizing, that he'd done something that *required* an apology. He normally wasn't this thick. He knew better than to bring up something serious when she was still a little high on the scene. He leaned down to her. Given her large personality, it was easy to forget he was much taller than she.

"Next time, we could take him to new heights ... together," he said. Watching her play had reduced all his defenses to ash. He questioned why he resisted his attraction to her at all. He was desperate to taste her lips again—hell, every part of her again.

"Together?"

"So coy, Sarah." He drew closer to her. God, she was stunning. Her tired eyes still alight. "Watching you tonight with Laurent ... We could be good together." He couldn't stop himself from pushing that possibility. He'd be a fool to ever stop trying.

She took in a breath that spoke of resignation, and her eyes drooped as if she was coming down a little. "We were

ELIZABETH SAFLEUR

once. But too much has happened. Our time has passed."
Before she could turn, his hand was around her delicate
bicep.

"Sarah."

She blinked up at him, and he tugged her closer. She
didn't turn her face away. Later, he would justify his next
move as being, perhaps not invited, but certainly not
rejected. He moved forward, and she did not yield the field—
not one bit, which only turned him on more. *Turned on.* How
about lit up inside like a rocket?

When he leaned down to get closer to her face, she
pressed his hands against his chest, and he stepped back—
one step.

"Tell you what. Don't interrupt a scene ever again," she
ground out.

"What are you talking about?"

"Asking my favorite part of a man. Then that stunt,
pressing yourself against me."

He retook that step he'd abdicated earlier. "I didn't hear
you complain."

"You didn't hear me comply."

He moved so close her breath touched his face.

"If you kiss me, be prepared for the consequences," she
said.

"I always am."

He wrapped his arms around her and pulled her in close,
obliterating every bit of space between them. He didn't kiss
her. Submissives weren't the only ones who needed aftercare,
and he let his instincts take over. Her feelings had ricocheted
too quickly. He recognized the signs of someone overtired,
and he hadn't helped by pressing matters and losing his
temper—*reacting* instead of understanding.

"What are you doing?" She twisted a little in his hold.

"Shhhh … let me." *Do this instead of what I want to do.* He

88

had enough control of his animalistic lust to know now was not the time to unleash the beast.

Her body softened under him, tension seeping from her shoulders first, then her rib cage. She drew in a long breath, but he didn't release his embrace until her face raised to his. For a long minute, he let himself get lost in her dark coffee-colored eyes. This time, when she tried to step back, he let her.

"I'll let you know when Laurent's ready to go home. The bar's still open downstairs." She slipped into her bedroom and shut him out.

*Jesus.* That night at Club 501 had been easy. Why? And, why is it hard now? He'd caught something in her eyes in the last few minutes. He finally recognized what it was. *Fear.* Sarah Marillioux was frightened? Scared of him? He could hardly entertain the thought. It tore at his heart a little, which was all that was needed for those dormant feelings for her to rush out so quickly he was forced to take in a long breath.

He often had to temper his urge to storm into a submissive's life, take over, make them talk, force his care on them. After all, it had to be their choice throughout to give themselves, including offering up their fears. It was the same with Dominants, but trickier. He wanted nothing more than to fling open that door and find out what had her so ... shielded all of a sudden. Yet, he couldn't take away her choice. Damn, he wasn't sure he could test, lure, or even *request* she face whatever it was that scared the hell out of her.

"We aren't done. Not by a long shot, Sarah," he said quietly to the closed door.

## 14

Laurent cracked open his eyes. Water ran somewhere in the distance. He shifted in the bed, muscles crying out at the movement. A wrench of metal and the whooshing of water stopped. He bolted upright and immediately regretted it. He was in Sarah Marillioux's room. Her perfume surrounded him. He kicked at the covers, though the fabric burned the welts on his ass. Last night he'd been flying so high he barely remembered how he got here. He'd wobbled and fallen into cool sheets and sank quickly into the darkness—sated, happy, peaceful.

His feet hit the carpet, and he stood, tentatively. It took less than a minute for his balance to restore, and he strode toward the bathroom, feeling the soreness from the scene. He loved reliving scenes through the sensations left by marks, bruises, and welts. Though he didn't display too many today, he'd never forget last night. He enjoyed the surprise of it the most—the fact they hadn't overly prepared for the play.

An ache started in his chest. Shit, he was coming down, that familiar depression creeping in as if everything was over with no hope of any more. Through the crack, he caught a mass of chestnut curls waterfalling off the back of a large, claw foot tub. *Sarah.* Just seeing her stopped that descent into hopelessness. He pushed the door open an inch, and she turned her head.

"Come in, Laurent." Her voice echoed slightly off the tiles. She twisted and draped an arm over the side. "Bring me that scrubber." She pointed to the countertop.

He stepped into the warm, humid air, and that ache dissipated in his chest instantly. He retrieved the blue mesh ball and knelt next to her.

"Wash my back." She leaned forward.

He dipped the scrubber into the milky water. He'd been right. She preferred a bath milk over bubbles. Slowly, starting in small circles, he ran the mesh ball over the smooth skin of her back. She curled forward, the bones of her spine protruding through her thin frame. If Steffan saw how thin she was, he'd be in his kitchen right now, spiraling out linguine from his pasta wheel.

He wet the sponge again and switched the direction of the circle caresses.

"Mmm. That's nice," she said.

He was ridiculously pleased that she enjoyed this small service. He could do so much more.

"How are you feeling?" she asked. "Are you sore? Feeling all right?"

"I feel great. I could have gone longer. Did Steffan stop us?"

"No."

He resumed running the mesh ball up and down her spine, slowly and gently. "He prefers to be involved," he explained.

"So he said." She turned back again in profile.

"I'd be fine if he joined us," he said tentatively. He wasn't sure if she enjoyed suggestions. "It's not that you're not enough. I would be honored to serve both of you. Whatever pleases you."

She leaned backward. "That's enough of my back."

"I can take much more than you know." He settled on his knees by the tub.

"It's not just about taking." She peered up at the ceiling. "It's vital you're clear about your limits."

"For me to be useless would be far worse than taking things too far. I don't … do well when I don't feel needed."

She drew out her arm and cupped his face. "Oh, Laurent, you do need looking after."

He turned his chin so he could press a chaste kiss in her palm. "Thank you, Mistress."

She smiled and dropped her hand. "Do something for me."

"Anything."

"Take a shower." She lifted her foot up from the milky water and pointed her big toe toward the corner glass shower. "Let me watch you."

He stood and padded over to the large blue-tiled shower. Americans and their space, he thought. He could live inside this glass box.

He wrenched on the water, let the steam rise and stepped inside. He unhooked a small squeegee hanging under the faucet and cleared the glass. She had said she wanted to watch. He wouldn't hinder her view of his wide-awake cock. Then perhaps she might allow him to serve her in other ways. His cock twitched in agreement with that possibility.

He squeezed a small amount of soap from a bottle in the corner, suds up his palms and lazily began to wash. She put her chin on her hands on the edge of the tub, and her dark brown eyes assessed him. Was she getting wet between her legs? His cock did another small dance at the thought.

"How's the water?" she asked.

"It's wonderful, but it'd be better if you were in here with me."

She chuckled. "I like that you say what you want, Laurent, but watching you will be all for today."

The hot water of the shower relaxed his muscles. The glass soon streaked with mist and fog again, and this time he didn't whisk it off. He turned and leaned against the glass, pressing his backside and shoulders firmly into the cool pane and almost reached for his cock. He resisted, but God, he'd give anything to come.

"Are you touching yourself, Laurent?"

His hands dropped to his sides, palms on either side of his hips and pressed them flat to the glass. "No, Mistress."

"Turn around."

He obeyed and slowly raised his eyes so he could see her —see her watching him, taking him in.

"Why didn't you?"

"You haven't given me permission, Mistress."

"That's right. And if you are going to be handling that big thing, I want to watch. Make yourself come for me. You'll do that for me, won't you?"

"Yes, Mistress. May I make you come?"

She smiled. "Another time. For now, you'll let me appreciate you. Show me, Laurent. Show me that glorious cock."

He reached for himself, giving his member one long stroke. "May I use soap?"

"Yes, and I want you to come hard for your Mistress. Don't hold anything back."

His insides lit up with her words. *Your Mistress.* He squeezed a healthy amount of the lilac-scented bath wash into his palm, foaming it between both hands before moving to his cock and balls. It took one long stroke for him to be impossibly hard. With Sarah's dark eyes glittering on the other side of the steamed glass, he wouldn't be surprised if he shot his come all over the shower wall with just one more pull. He drew in lungfuls of thick muggy air, as the water hit his backside, igniting the welts and bruises from last night. He *was* going to come hard.

"Mistress?"

"Yes, now," she mouthed.

He let himself go, a long spurt hitting the glass between them.

Her lips drew up in a slow, wide smile. She then winked. "You may get out now. Steffan texted me while you were sleeping. He's wondering about you, and waiting downstairs."

"Has he been waiting long?" He turned off the water.

"Yes, he has."

He cracked open the door and reached for a fluffy white towel. "You're angry with him."

"No. I'm not."

"He trusts you—more than I've ever seen him trust anyone else."

"He can. I would never harm you."

"I know that."

"Do you?" Her eyes grew fierce.

"Of course. Steffan's judgment is impeccable. Then there was our scene ..." His cock might never stand down again. She noticed. He cleared his throat. "I sensed ... something."

"Steffan and I have history, as you know." She stood suddenly, soap bubbles running a trail down her skin. Jesus, the woman was thin, but her full breasts were firm, the long muscles in her legs pronounced, and ... He ripped his gaze away. He'd been gawking. She reached for a towel hanging on a heat rack by the side of the tub.

"I'm sorry. I shouldn't have mentioned anything." He dropped his own towel and ran to assist her, helped her out of the tub.

"Not at all." She gave him a forced smile. "There's nothing to tell, really. You were there at Club 501, watching us, correct? We had a wonderful weekend together, as I have had with many men."

"I think Steffan would like … more. You were good together." He should not have said that, but it was part of this whole plan—to get all three of them together. He had to push a little even if it meant angering the woman he could easily become addicted to.

"You'd think wrong then, Laurent," she said quietly. "And, you are not to gossip about me to him or about him to me. Understand?"

"Of course."

Her admonishment cut him bone-deep, mostly because he'd have to obey her now when all he wanted to do was delve deep into what was wrong between them. Something was definitely off. She and Steffan were friendly with one another, but she didn't trust him. Perhaps she felt something around Steffan—had or still did—and it troubled her enough to hold herself back when it came to him. He knew one thing, she intrigued Steffan more than any woman he'd seen.

She wrapped the towel around her, depriving him of those exquisite breasts, swells of succulent flesh he could worship for hours.

"Now, let's not keep him waiting any longer. I'm not a sadist." She cupped his cheek. "And, keeping you from anyone would be cruel."

"Are you sure I can't do … more for you?" His hard-on was up for any job she required.

She ran her gaze over his body. "Perhaps another time."

Shit, he was going to have to up his game here.

## 15

"Thank you for asking me to lunch." Steffan shook Alexander's hand.

"Thank you for bringing some of your homemade bread. No one bakes anymore, and it's a pity." Alexander lowered himself into the large chair, and Steffan took the opposite place. They had a stunning view of the gardens from the large window to their left.

Alexander's office was predictably grand—mahogany paneled walls, bookshelves with first-edition classics, and an imposing desk dominating the center of space. He wondered how many people had been summoned—for that's clearly was what this was—to the man's private dining nook in this office. Two steps inside the door and Steffan decided he would feel honored rather than intimidated.

"Your gardens are spectacular." Steffan snapped his napkin into place, and a stunning blond woman wearing nothing but a gold rope dress poured water into large blue goblets. "And your help, beautiful."

"Luna? Master Steffan paid you a compliment," Alexander said.

"Thank you, Master Steffan." She bowed her head and backed up.

"It's important for everyone to feel appreciation, even the tops," Alexander explained. "I hope you like crab cakes. Being so close to the Chesapeake Bay, we get the finest crab meat."

"Sounds wonderful."

Alexander nodded at Luna who slipped out the door. He ripped a large piece of bread off the rosemary loaf Steffan had brought.

"We're assessing your application to Accendos next week." Alexander forked a lettuce leaf from his salad.

He'd learned most people at Accendos got to the point quickly, something he appreciated. "Good. We're eager to get settled. You know how it is."

"Yes, and I see Sarah has moved things along from the other evening. Things go well?" He took a large bite of his bread and murmured an appreciation.

"Laurent was quite happy." Steffan smiled.

Alexander chuckled. "Yes, Sarah certainly knows her way around men. After you first called, I spoke with Sarah about you. The two of you know each other."

"Our time together was brief, but I'm glad you talked about us. I was wondering if you'd be willing to answer a few questions about her."

"About Sarah?" Alexander leaned back in his chair.

"Yes, and, I hope it won't go any further than these four walls."

"Members are expelled for sharing personal information about each other. Discretion and respect for people's privacy are principles strictly enforced for all club members. I am not exempt." Alexander gazed at him steadily and continued in a gentle, cultured voice that carried little emotion. "I've been in this scene longer than most here. I came up during a time when secrecy wasn't just preferred; it was vital to one's survival. The 1970s were very different from today's environment for those of us in our special community."

"I can imagine."

"It was an unkind time. My experiences are one of the reasons I opened Accendos and launched the Tribunal Council. First, here in Washington and then spreading to dozens of other cities. But you know all that, I trust."

"It's one of the reasons why Laurent and I are here. And I believe it's only fair I know more about the person who is exploring my best friend. After all, seven Tribunal Council members are about to dig deep into my and Laurent's life."

"It's fair." Alexander lifted his water glass. "Anything you say to me is 100% confidential."

"Thank you." He picked up his salad fork and took a large bite of cucumber. He required a second to assess where to start. He'd go for the punchline. "Sarah is different than I recall."

"How so?"

"More guarded. Rigid. And tired."

The door cracked open, and Luna stepped back inside, balancing two plates on her arm. After settling the crab cakes before them, she disappeared as silently as she had entered. The scent of fresh crab reminded him of home and a slight, odd sense of wishing for the familiar arose. Washington had not been as easy as he'd hoped. Sarah certainly hadn't been.

He'd woken up and lay in bed with a hard-on the size of a rolling pin after remembering how she'd worked over Laurent. He'd also woken up with clarity over what came next. He wanted to pick up where they'd left off two years ago. Her dismissal of him last night—that's what he decided he saw in her eyes—only ratcheted up his resolve. He couldn't believe he'd misread the interest she had in him in London. As for Laurent? He complicated matters.

"Sarah works too hard," Alexander said.

"She's without a partner," he said. "Do you know why?"

Alexander leaned back and chortled. "Have a crush do we? Well, don't feel too bad, my man. Greater men than you have fallen in Sarah's presence."

"I'm going to lay out my cards here. I am interested in a long-term relationship with her. Whatever she decides on that front, I can handle. If she wants to keep it brief, okay. I won't like it, but it won't ruin the rest of my life. Laurent, however, doesn't do short-term well. If he should fall in love, I'd like to know she'd be careful with him."

The man stilled. "How much do you know about Sarah's past? What has she told you about her beginnings here?"

"Nothing."

"I'm afraid I can't enlighten you much, but I can tell you she didn't start out in the scene here. We met in a public play space in a club in the Southwest some years ago. She was getting over someone. Someone she believes she hurt."

"She hurt?" He couldn't imagine such a thing. She was so careful.

"That's why she is adamant on having structure and rules. I've known her for twelve years now, and I can tell you that she is the safest Dominant you can find. Next to me, of course." There was no arrogance in Alexander's voice, but rather a conviction that made Steffan believe the man. "She doesn't make mistakes, Steffan. I can assure you that. Laurent will be in fine hands."

"I made a mistake." There he'd said it, and yes, it felt as humiliating as it sounded.

Alexander assessed him. "Am I going to regret asking what you did? She told me you once scened together."

"It was more than that. Much more."

"I see."

"And, both being Dominants makes it more difficult." That was the truth. The way she'd relaxed in his arms ... He'd

ELIZABETH SAFLEUR

wanted to capture her lips, push her against the wall, and ravage her. He'd held himself back, but he wouldn't be able to do so forever.

"Sarah also can be overly cautious," Alexander said. "Sometimes she lets the past infect too much of the future— especially for herself." Alexander eyed him. "You care for her."

"It's hard not to." Another truth.

"Over the years I have learned to trust my instincts. When I mentioned you, for a moment, she looked rattled. I suspect you once got under her skin, and that, my friend, is something I have rarely seen. You also should know I'd do anything for Sarah. She's important to me." His warning was clear.

'If you're wondering if my intentions are pure—"

"I'm sure they are, but hurt comes in many forms."

"That sounds like something Laurent would say. He also says everyone must be true to themselves or life's not worth living."

"Wise man."

"He's the best."

"How do you like your crab?"

"Makes me feel like I'm home."

"Perhaps you are."

He could only hope. After this "chat" with Alexander, he may not have understood more about Sarah, but he now knew he was going to have to be more direct with her. She was going to have to reject him outright to get rid of him.

# 16

"Gorgeous." Master R took a sip of espresso. His eyes never left Charlotte. Sarah's choice for the woman's collaring ceremony dress *was* perfect.

"You really like it?" Charlotte ran her hands down the pale yellow fabric, the drapes of material rippling under her hands.

"Not many people can carry off this color, but against your red hair, it's stunning," Sarah said.

Her Master stood. "The question is, Charlotte, do you like it?"

Charlotte's self-confidence, once shattered from an abusive upbringing and then the untimely death of her husband, hadn't been easy to restore. Master R had done remarkably well with her. She wasn't as confident as Laurent, but ... *Damn-it.* Sarah couldn't get him out of her mind—and Steffan. The man had pulled her into an embrace —something she hadn't invited but hadn't completely hated, either. It was sweet if she thought about it. He couldn't leave her alone, though, could he? He had to look down on her, his lips parting as if he was going to kiss her. She wasn't crossing that line. She wouldn't let *him* cross that line.

"Yes, sir. I love it." Charlotte's voice hitched.

"Then, good. You shall have it," he declared.

"Let's get you out of this." Sarah unzipped the hidden zipper. After Charlotte stepped out, wearing nothing but a tiny thong, she stood unabashed in front of everyone. The girl may lack confidence around some things, but her body was not one of them. Charlotte was a flagrant exhibitionist and who could blame her?

"Madeline, please box up the dress for Charlotte." She handed her assistant the garment and turned to the young girl. "You will look like a princess at your ceremony."

Charlotte nervously clutched her hands but did little to hide her breasts. "I just want to appeal to my … you." She'd stopped herself from saying *Master*.

"You could be wearing a potato sack, and I'd still slay dragons for a taste of this." He bent down, tipped her chin up with one finger and lightly touched his lips to hers.

Their display was a little over the top, but it was nice to see such honest love. All that connected energy coursing between them softened her a little on the inside. She was usually content with helping people find love and happiness in her own way—like flogging a delicious Spanish hunk with hazel eyes that appeared lit from the inside. She'd pleasured herself many times recalling the way Laurent swayed in his bonds, the way he handled his cock in her shower. The fact Steffan's face came up as well was a little irritating, but nothing she couldn't deal with.

While Master R and Charlotte continued to stare at one another dreamily, Sarah sidled up to her assistant.

"Madeline, who do we have on the docket next?"

"It's four o'clock, Sarah. No one."

"Four already?" Damn, she wasn't ready to go home, and

she certainly wasn't going to go to Accendos—far too dangerous. According to her sources, Steffan and Laurent had practically moved in. She needed a little time to regroup from the other evening.

While Madeline helped Charlotte back into her T-shirt and jeans, she scrolled through her appointment book on her iPad. There had to be messages to return or perhaps she'd start the next charity event. There were so many causes that could use her help.

"Oh, excuse me, sir," a familiar male voice said. She turned and found Laurent holding a large bouquet of white roses and a white paper bag. He stepped backward to let Master R and Charlotte pass through the door. Outside light haloed his dark curls, giving him an angelic appearance—as if he needed anything else to remind her of his unearthly charisma.

"Laurent," she said. "What brings you here?"

"I hope you don't mind me popping in. I don't have your number, and I didn't want to ask …" His voice trailed off. He strode forward and held out the bouquet. "For you. To thank you. I can put them in water." His eyes darted around.

"How kind. Roses." Her mind immediately recalled using the rose flogger on him. "Madeline can put these in water."

"And, Steffan's homemade cinnamon rolls." He held up a wrinkled white paper bag. "Once you taste them, you'll never have any others."

She took the flowers from him.

"They are my new favorite flowers since …" He shrugged, and his full lips stretched into a smile, little crinkles forming around his eyes. His olive roll-neck sweater brought out the green in his eyes, and those Boss pants—she recognized them from last year's collection—hugged him in all the right places. He could have been a man about to go to the gentleman's club for a Sunday afternoon of reading The Times.

"Wow. Tiger of Sweden." He set the bag on a chair and strode over to the garment rack holding the new line of men's wear that arrived yesterday.

"You know this line?"

"Yes, a little snug for my taste, but this ... may I?" He pointed to a particular jacket.

After setting down the flowers, she strode over and pulled out the new 1903 suit jacket. "Good eye." She held it up against him. "Yes. Turn around." She held it up so he could slip it on. He immediately shrugged it up to his broad shoulders and turned around.

"Well?"

"Come." She held out her hand and led him to the podium surrounded by three-way mirrors. He took the center placement.

"Nice stitching here." He held up a cuff.

"Yes, very nice," She wasn't talking about the jacket. She'd noted his perfect proportions before, but now she understood how perfect. The jacket hung on him like a custom-made hanger.

"You ever model?" she asked.

He laughed. "Hang out with all those divas? No, thank you."

She could see it, though—Laurent striding up a runway with that I-don't-care stance and a sexy I-know-something-you-don't simper on his face.

His face fell suddenly.

"What's wrong? Don't like it?" she asked.

"It's perfect, but I came here to ..." He shrugged out of the jacket and stepped off his pedestal. His eyes landed on Madeline who'd returned with a tray bearing two demitasse cups. The rich aroma of espresso reached them.

"I thought perhaps you could use a little pick-me-up." She

smiled at Sarah conspiratorially, her eyes darting between her and Laurent.

"Thank you, Madeline. Would you put those roses in water for me? Then you can go for the day." She purposefully evened out her voice. Madeline saw entirely too much of her life already.

Her assistant put the tray down on a small table, not hiding her appreciation of Laurent as she made her way out. Sarah understood how Steffan might feel when out and about with Laurent. He was a people magnet.

She took the jacket from Laurent and rehung it in its place. When she turned, Laurent held out one of the small cups. "Could we talk?" he asked, hesitantly.

She nodded.

They settled themselves on two chairs where the mothers of brides and uncomfortable husbands had sat a hundred times and sipped their java. Her stomach grumbled, and he darted up to retrieve the bag he'd abandoned. He pulled out a large cinnamon bun that smelled divine.

"May I?" He lifted a knife.

"Please."

"Thank you for taking a break for me." Using the tray as a plate, he sank the knife through the middle of a bun that oozed white cream cheese frosting. She really shouldn't, but had she remembered to have lunch?

"Now what brings you here? You're all right, aren't you?" Subs often dropped after a scene, sometimes the after effects showing up days later.

"I'm wonderful. I very much enjoyed our time together the other night."

"As did I."

"Did you?" Worry dripped from those two simple words. "Did you and Steffan argue?"

"Is that what he told you?"

"No, I know Steffan—well, and he's … not himself."

"We did not argue. Now, will you please cut me a small piece?" She dipped her head toward the cinnamon bun.

After drawing the fork through the corner of the bun, he brought it to her mouth. She shook her head. She took the fork from him and plucked it off the tines.

"Open." He opened his lips, and she placed the frosted morsel on his tongue. Before she could withdraw her fingers, he closed his soft lips over them. Her thumb raked over his bottom teeth and lip—the opposing sensations of hard enamel and wet flesh igniting the arousal that had simmered under the surface of her consciousness the last few days.

"Naughty boy," she said softly.

His mouth moved in a sensual way as he chewed the piece of cinnamon bun. "What can I do to make it up to you?" he asked.

She leaned back. This distance she'd put between them hadn't dimmed her desire for him one iota.

"Cut me another piece," she directed.

He did as she asked and speared it with the fork. He offered the sinful morsel to her. She drew off the piece and placed it in her mouth. The sugar burst over her tongue, the pleasure almost orgasmic.

"Mmmm." She wiped her tongue over her bottom lip to capture the final taste. Steffan *could* bake, and that fact shouldn't have intrigued her so.

"I thought you'd like them." He stared at her lips. "Steffan had to go out of town. New York."

"Oh?"

"I mean if you're wondering why you haven't heard from him."

"I'm not." She placed her hand on his wrist, and he stilled. "Laurent, knees."

He slipped from his chair and settled himself before her.

Hands, palm up, on his thighs, he bent his neck in a genuine reverence.

"Look at me." She purposefully did not touch him when he obeyed. "I'm very glad you came to me, but I'm going to say this once. You don't have to worry about anything that happens between Steffan and I. Two Doms butting heads is as common as clouds. It has nothing to do with you."

"So you and Steffan did argue."

She shouldn't have let that slip. Worse, her rising irritation irked her. She was better than this. "Laurent, cut me another small piece."

He expertly cut another small corner of the cinnamon bun and held it out to her. She took it from him with her fingers, and her stomach immediately let off an unladylike grumble. She chuckled. "Okay, perhaps I skipped breakfast, too."

"Steffan can cook for you," Laurent said. "He makes his own sauces and homemade bread."

"Talented." She licked sugar off her fingers, his eyes trained on her mouth.

"And, a good man, Mistress Sarah."

"I know, Laurent. You two have unprecedented loyalty to one another."

"He's the most loyal person I've known."

"I'm sure you are the same." She really didn't want to talk about Steffan any longer. The last few days, she'd worked to organize her memories of his warmth, his scent and put them in their proper place. She determined she could *admire* him as a fellow Dom. She could *not* get romantic notions.

"Now, I could use your help. Please rise." She stood, and he immediately joined her. "Care to model some of the pieces for me? I'd like to put some outfits together."

"Mistress Sarah, I would like nothing better. Well, except …"

"I'm afraid I left my handcuffs at home."

"Pity."

She laughed, feeling rather good about their conversation. Laurent had a talent for smoothing things over, perhaps? Had things needed to be smoothed over? Hadn't *he* needed reassuring? Their roles moved back and forth like liquid—the power of taking care of one another shifting back and forth like sand rolling under an ocean wave. It felt nice. Responsibility was a heavy load, and being with Laurent was so easy, unlike Steffan. She wished she'd known he was out of town. She could have had Laurent here like this, all to herself, without anything in the way of getting to know the man.

"Laurent, when did you say school started?"

"In a few months."

Hmmm, a little time. She rather liked having Laurent around more, so she made another instinctive move when it came to him.

"What do you think about coming to work for me until then?"

## 17

Sarah's good feelings from her time with Laurent lasted through two hours of fitting Laurent with Armani, vintage Pierre Cardin, Gucci—all wrong for him—and Brunello Cucinelli. Those positive vibes lasted through the drive home, through a sudden spring thunderstorm that slowed traffic to a crawl and choked the streets with tentative drivers. They only vanished when her headlights illuminated her front door. Christiana stood huddled under the portico of her front entrance, water running in sheets off her red raincoat.

"Christiana, what's wrong?"

The girl's cheeks were wet and not only with rain.

Sarah got the door open, abandoned her umbrella, and pushed the young girl inside.

"I took the metro." Christiana's teeth chattered as she tiptoed in, water splashing on to the hardwood floor, her arms hugging her chest.

"That's five blocks away." She threw off her own coat, yanked a shawl off a nearby chair and threw it around the shivering girl. Her sneakers squeaked on the floor as Sarah placed her in the entrance hall chair.

She wrestled the girl's sneakers off. "Let me get a towel."

She padded to the bathroom and back, bringing a stack of towels the maids had laid out for her. She dried the young girl's feet.

"What's going on?"

Her answer was a sob—a burst of emotion that sat Sarah back on her heels. At the same time, Christiana's phone buzzed in her hand. She hadn't noticed she'd been holding it.

"Tha-that's Jonathan," she said.

Sarah took it from her and answered.

"Christiana, tell me—" his voice was angry, pained.

"Jay, it's me, Sarah. She's here with me."

The sound of a relieved expelling of breath carried through the phone. "What the hell is going on? I've been calling for an hour."

"Where are you?"

"Hell if I know. Probably somewhere over Kansas."

"You're on a plane?" That explained the loud whooshing sound.

She rose from her crouch.

"On my way to San Francisco, and the second we land, I'm taking the return flight."

She rested a hand on Christiana's shoulder. "I'm handing you over to …"

Christiana shook her head violently and mouthed *please*.

"To Christiana." She held out the phone. "Talk to him, love. Then we'll talk."

The girl tentatively took the phone and held it to her ear. "Hi," she said and then started to cry again. Sarah couldn't hear what Jonathan was saying, but it was clearly the right thing, as her face softened. She chewed on a fingernail … and continued to listen. She nodded, which made Sarah chuckle a little as Jonathan couldn't see a thing. But strong emotion often did that—removed one's sense of, well, anything.

Christiana finally spoke. "You don't have to do that. My phone battery will die before you land. No. really. Talking to me on an airplane has to be costing you a fortune ... Of course you didn't ... Okay." She took a deep breath and straightened. "I love you, too." She handed the phone to Sarah. "He wants to talk to you."

She took it and turned her back, striding into the living room. "That was fast."

"She needed to be reassured, that's all. Sarah, please keep her with you. She ran into Avery."

The sound of that name stiffened her insides. "Avery *Churchill*? Where?" Christiana shuddered a little at her bark. How could Avery, who put a bullet into Jonathan three years ago, who'd gotten off scot-free thanks to an insanity plea, be *out* on her own? Last time she'd heard, the girl was in a mental facility for the criminally insane several states away.

"Massachusetts Avenue," he said. "I didn't tell you, but—"

"Tell me what?" She walked deeper into the living room— as far away from her future sister-in-law as she could. When she thought back to that time when they'd all almost lost him ... she shuddered. She couldn't imagine what seeing the woman did to Christiana.

"Avery was released a year ago. Now, please do me a favor. Make Christiana talk about it, Sarah. I'll be there in eight hours. I'm taking a jet back."

A stupid laugh burst through her lips. "You're talking about the woman who *shot* you, Jay," she said in an angry whisper. A shock of pain ripped through her body at remembering the phone call she'd gotten from Mark, his driver and assistant at the time. Jonathan had recovered, but to this day Sarah held her breath whenever she saw any news related to gunshots on the news.

"Avery is now married to my former assistant, Shane. She also wears an ankle monitor, or so I'm told. I didn't tell Christiana that I knew all this, so when she called me in a panic, and I didn't panic back …" He let out a long breath.

"You don't panic."

"I might be now. We had an argument, and she's already stressed to the max. Sarah, I'm begging you." The steel in his voice made it sound more like a command—the only man who could get away with it in her world. She loved her step-brother, and there was no way she was letting Christiana out of her sight until Jonathan got there.

"Sarah, she's not going to want to talk at first. Press it. If she doesn't, it'll fester—fast. Maybe you can find out what else is eating her. It's not just the wedding, Claire, the colors, hell, even this. It's like she's afraid to move us forward." He sighed. "She won't tell me, but I know it's there."

It was huge for Jonathan to admit his failure to get the love of his life to confess her true feelings.

"Jay, you'll need to get to the bottom of this yourself."

"I will when I get there. Don't let her bolt."

"I won't." She killed the call.

She returned to Christiana. Her hands wedged under her thighs, the young woman rocked back and forth a little and stared at her bare feet.

"Christiana, let's get you out of those wet clothes."

"What?" She looked up at her. "Oh, sure."

She led the girl to her bathroom, stripped her of her sopping wet jeans and t-shirt—no easy feat. The girl really did need a wardrobe boost. She wrapped her in a fluffy white robe and got her situated on her couch with a mug of hot tea. Sarah texted her dinner companion that she'd have to reschedule their meeting and then settled in for the vigil.

"Christiana." She finally steeled her voice to the Dominant she knew would get the girl's attention.

Christiana lifted her gaze from studying her tea as if divining a prophecy from the tea leaves. "He told you to make me talk, didn't he?" She sighed. "I've never met a man who liked to talk so much."

"He's a good Dominant."

Her eyes misted with tears again. "He's the best, and contrary to what it looks like around my wedding disinterest, I love him with all my heart."

"Of course you do. Now, why don't you start at the beginning?"

Her chin wobbled, but then she stilled and pulled all her emotion inside—something Sarah had seen Christiana do often. Something big was going down, and if she knew anything it was this: Christiana and Jonathan were ordained by divinity to be together.

"Avery was pushing a baby carriage. A frickin' baby carriage." A sense of incredulity had crept into Christiana's voice. "Can you believe *that*? I was so *pissed*."

Good, anger was better than grief, especially when talking about that woman.

"I can imagine."

"I mean, I finally had the chance to confront her. Slap the shit out of her, and there she was with a … *baby* carriage. A real, live, gorgeous baby. I sneaked a look. I'm talking Gerber commercial level."

"And that made you angry?"

"No, it was like it all dissolved. Avery practically ran away from me, as if she was scared of me. It was bizarre. I tried to follow but the carriage was bouncing, and I didn't want to hurt the baby. I wanted to talk to her. I wanted to know why … how … I mean, a *baby*! The woman starved herself through high school so her stomach was concave. Avery got out her phone and spoke to someone rapidly. I heard the name Shane. So when I called Jonathan, he told me Avery and

Shane—his former assistant—got married. He knew and hadn't told me, Sarah! I mean, he should have told me."

"I'm sure he wanted to spare you."

"He doesn't need to *spare* me. He needs to stop treating me like I'm made of spun glass. I know I haven't made it easy by freaking out about the wedding, and now, I'm freaking out about Avery. You know the worst part? He said he wants children. Like right away." Her mouth dropped open. "Us. I mean, I have just run into Avery Churchill, and he pops out with 'I want kids.' Guess what? I may not want kids. Like at all." She sliced the air with her hand.

She now understood why Jonathan had been adamant about Christiana talking. Once the girl got going she certainly had a lot to say—and honest words, albeit a little mixed up.

"You might change your mind about having children."

"I doubt it. I didn't have the best mother role models."

"Who has?"

"Isabella," she said quickly. "I love her mom. She's bossy but in a caring way. I love it when she brushes my bangs from my face. I know they annoy her. Sometimes I let them hang so she does it."

Sarah could see Christiana doing that, having been so neglected in her childhood. She'd want someone to pay attention to her even if it was to correct her.

"You're like that, too," Christiana said. "You're always straightening the seams on my tops."

"I'm a stylist. It's what I do."

"But you only do it to me outside a fitting. Don't get me wrong. I like it." Color tinged her cheeks. "It's like you care."

"I do care about you, Christiana. Deeply." A tickle that presaged tears formed in her throat.

"Didn't your mother do that to you, growing up? Fuss? I can totally see it …" She snorted.

"Not like you think. My mother was intent on me getting married as quickly as possible. She wanted me to dress up so I'd appeal to men." Early and often, she thought bitterly. She pushed aside that recurring thought that Claire was more pimp than mother, but this wasn't the time to revisit old resentments.

Sarah returned her focus to Christiana. "Then turn to Marie Santos or me when you have questions. You know we're all family by choice right?"

She nodded. "I don't know what I'd do without all of you. I don't know what I *did*—before Jonathan."

*Oh, to be so in love you can't imagine what your life was like without that other person.*

"Can I ask you something personal?" Christiana's voice was tentative. "Don't you want someone—for yourself? You're so good at taking care of others. I mean don't you want 'The One'?" She leaned her head back on the couch and looked up at the ceiling. "Someone who seizes you and kisses you and you just *know*?"

She chuckled. "Is that what Jonathan did to you?"

Christiana raised her head. "In the ladies' bathroom in the Russell Senate Building."

Sarah laughed more heartily despite that gnawing around her heart. So much love swirled around Christiana it was going to kill Sarah—and not in a jealous way but in its truth about the young girl's courage—something that, for the first time in her life, Sarah was beginning to doubt she had. It was an unnerving thought for someone who spent her days dominating others.

"More tea?" she asked, more to change the subject than anything else.

"Yes, please."

When Sarah returned, Christiana had fallen fast asleep. Sarah pulled the blanket up around her shoulders and sat with her until Jonathan arrived, hours later. He marched out her front door, his young fiancé curled asleep in his arms, and a whispered thank you on his lips. She'd merely shaken her head and smiled at him. They didn't need to talk. Like he and Christiana, she and Jonathan had a silent understanding between them that transcended speech.

Sarah curled up in a blanket on her couch and stared out at the blush of pink that slowly spread over the cement gray sky as morning peeked over the treetops. She gave her imagination free rein to consider what it would be like to be so in love you'd charter a private jet to return you to your lover because you couldn't bear for her to cry alone. Would she do that for Laurent? Would he for her? Steffan had said Laurent wanted to belong to someone. What would Steffan do then? Go back to Sweden? There would be no reason for him to stay.

# 18

Steffan threw his keys on the small table inside the doorway and stretched his arms back. He could use a drink, though it'd likely make him fall asleep on his feet. He'd had to run up to New York for a quick overnight trip, and the rain over the last day had delayed his return.

He did a double take at the couch encased in plastic in the center of the room.

"Laurent," he called.

"Well? You get it?" Laurent strode through the archway leading to the kitchen.

"The grant went through. $250K." He pointed to the new couch. "Brown, huh?"

"Apparently the color is back in."

Steffan strode over to the long sectional couch and sank down, the plastic crackling under his weight. "Comfortable. You work fast." He indicated the large painting of three horses against a turquoise blue sky. "Not bad." Steffan had to admit the artwork was good—not gaudy but not without life.

"I stopped by Sarah's office yesterday. She said Dante is an up and coming artist. I thought you'd like it."

"I do. So, did Sarah invite you over?" He'd been thinking about Sarah for days. Couldn't shake his brain of her image. If he hadn't had to run up to New York for this meeting, he'd have been tempted to reach out to her.

"Nope. Made a surprise visit."

"Ballsy. How'd that work out?"

"Envious?" Laurent plopped down next to him and put his feet, ankles crossed, on yet another new piece of furniture, an iron and glass coffee table.

"Of what? Of being put on my knees for showing up unannounced?" It was a wild guess, but he'd have done it if any of the luscious little things he'd been with had popped into his workplace. By the color on Laurent's face, he'd guessed correctly.

"What'd she make you do? Pick lint off the floor with your teeth?" he asked.

"She offered me a job."

He scratched the side of his neck. *Well played, Sarah Marillioux.* He'd stepped backward the last few days to allow things to settle, to see what Sarah might do next. Consequently, it was Laurent who made the next move. Okay, fine. Seemed to work. Sarah responded to him, but now she'd changed the game by bringing Laurent into her personal life —something she'd seemed vehemently opposed to. It wasn't the first time he'd see Laurent crack through someone's walls, have them act uncharacteristically.

"Luring you away from school?" He could appreciate that Sarah was getting to know Laurent outside of Accendos, but he didn't want Laurent to lose himself completely, or, have boundaries overstepped, such as allowing him to forget why he came to Washington in the first place.

"Nah. It's part-time. Assisting her with Christiana and Jonathan's wedding—guests who wouldn't mind the occasional reference to Accendos. She said her male clients often prefer other men in the room, that it calms their ruffled male egos at having to try on clothes."

"So, you like her," Steffan said.

"I do. She likes you, too. I think she just doesn't know what to do with you."

"Believe me, the feeling's mutual."

"The three of us could be good together. We could help her. She needs … something. Can't put my finger on it."

"Yes." *Truth.*

"The Tribunal is making a decision about us this afternoon," Laurent said. "I overheard her talking on her phone."

"Eavesdropping? Good man. I'm glad the Tribunal is making a decision. It's about time." He instantly got a second wind. "Hey, you get the groceries?" He'd texted Laurent that morning with a long list. His friend needed to stay occupied, and he supposed Sarah was helping him there with this "job."

"Yep. We feeding an army?"

"What do you say to bringing Sarah dinner at Accendos? Interested?"

"Always interested."

He rose. Action, that's what Steffan needed now. Her recent move had the gears in his brain turning. Time to put the second piece of the puzzle in place. Current wisdom said Dominants attempting to couple would only sentence themselves to a relentless tug-of-war for power. Steffan wasn't about to be lured into something he couldn't control, but he also wasn't one to follow popular dogma that stood in the way of what he wanted.

He headed to the kitchen. A nice Moroccan stew should do nicely. Exhilaration replaced his earlier fatigue. There was more to life than work, and it was time to stop hesitating. Time to inject himself into the equation.

## 19

"These are for you. From Laurent." Carrie held out a large glass vase overflowing with classic, red roses as soon as Sarah stepped from the Tribunal Council meeting room.

"And another one falls," Derek laughed behind her. "Wait 'til Steffan does, too."

Carson gave a rare chuckle as he strode by. "Two Doms together? I'd have to see that to believe it."

"Like I said in the meeting, Steffan and I have played together before," Sarah said matter-of-factly and pulled out a note tucked between the center blooms. She'd learned from Jonathan, the ex-politician, the surest way to stop gossip was to put the truth out front and center.

The Club Accendos memberships for Laurent and Steffan had passed unanimously. She had known they would. Their dossier was so thick it made an audible thud when it had hit the table. No one could question their level of experience in the scene—together and apart. She smothered that nip of jealousy—so unlike her—that appeared when Derek had joked about the number of clubs Steffan, in particular, had mesmerized. After all, she'd had plenty of men and on her terms.

"Can you put these in my room, Carrie?" She plucked one long stem from the center of the bouquet before Carrie spirited it away. She opened the note and stared at the elegant scrawl across the stiff white paper.

*Dungeon after the meeting? It's not Morocco. It's better.*

"They've been waiting for an hour," Carrie said over her shoulder.

She looked up to find herself alone with Alexander, the last to leave the meeting.

"An hour …" Alexander chuckled. "Good of him to warn you this time."

"If this counts as a warning." She folded the paper and sighed. "Quite presumptuous, don't you think? Their membership might not have passed."

"Yet it did." He eyed her. "Sarah, you know I don't tell people what to do in their personal lives."

"But?"

"You may want to test these waters. Steffan is interested in you. Now you need to decide if you're interested." He pecked her on the cheek and turned away, ending any more discussion. What would she have said anyway?

She ran her finger along the edge of the paper. When she pictured Laurent, blood rushed faster in her veins. She did something then she'd refused to allow herself since Steffan had pulled her into that unexpected embrace. She shut her eyes and remembered when she'd first seen his ice blue eyes turn violet in those red lights at Club 501. God help her, desire soared up her torso and cascaded down her spine like lava from a volcano at the thought of reliving that night in London. She placed the rose petals to her nose and turned to the stairs leading to the basement.

Steffan leaned against the large etching of the dragon in the doorway, its wide wingspan showing on either side of him. Laurent knelt beside him. Muted red light, like that night in Club 501, washed the hallway. She had the odd thought she was viewing a living version of a Thomas Stothard painting. She couldn't tell if Steffan was the devil from *Satan Summoning His Legions,* where the stunning blond devil called his followers forth. Or, perhaps he reminded her of the angel in the artist's *A Midsummer's Night Dream,* where the shining angel bestowed a smile on the mortals gathered around his feet. From the lopsided grin he wore, he could be assuming either role.

"We've been waiting for you. Brought you dinner." He lifted a cloth market bag.

She held up his note. "So you said. What did you bring?" The spicy, savory smell filling the hallway was divine.

"Moroccan stew. Good dish to help celebrate." He handed the bag to Laurent.

"Awfully sure of yourself."

He pushed off the wall and shoved both hands in his pockets. "No more games, Sarah. Laurent wants you. I want you. Was it so bad two years ago?"

"No, it wasn't."

"So, what do you say? I owe Laurent a reward. Remember?"

"Sharing a woman. I remember."

"And Laurent won't go in without you."

She examined Laurent's upturned face.

"You've spoiled me for anyone else," he said.

Those words were flattering, alluring, and to Sarah, they signaled death. Painful memories of the past lurked like a succubus that could suck her lifeforce. How do you tell someone—two beautiful someones—who'd offered themselves that they shouldn't have?

"Whatever is holding you back from taking this gift, let it

go." Steffan's voice, edged in a mix of compassion and command straightened her spine. She hadn't lied when she said Steffan was a good Dom. Yet, she didn't need to be topped. She needed absolution—something that would never come for her.

He looked up at the ceiling and back at her. "Red lights. Remember?"

"I remember everything." That was what made him so dangerous.

Affection warmed his eyes at her words.

Well, the man had brought her food—maybe he could exorcize demons for a few moments. She took the bag from Laurent. "How about eating later?"

She stepped to the dungeon door and placed her hand on the door lever. Turning back now wasn't possible. She couldn't resist their allure. Her erect posture sagged for a moment before she re-armed herself and straightened. "I said no promises. Take what I offer and don't ask me for what I can't give." She swung open the door.

## 20

Sarah exuded a devastating self-confidence, but twice now, Steffan had gotten a taunting glimpse at a hole in her otherwise impregnable persona. Something had happened to her which he would uncover—later. For now, she was here. He was justified in pushing. Sarah wasn't prone to ask for help, and his gut told him she needed it. She needed *them*. Another pompous thought, but whatever.

They'd done little talking after they'd first entered the room—a spartan space lined in mirrors with a concrete floor and recessed lights in shades of blue and red. Hard-looking metal grids with various bondage points ranged across its ceiling. She'd called for Carrie who whisked her dinner away, something he'd have to address with her later. Her lack of eating wasn't healthy. Still, he'd let her set the stage, first by placing Laurent in the center of the room, then by waiting for her to choose the type of play they'd engage in. It hadn't taken her long to choose.

Laurent, nude, stood under an impressive latticed grid she'd lowered from the ceiling. She circled him. His hair shone a dark purple in the crimson spotlight. His hands curled around one thick chain that hung overhead, and his cock jutted forward in anticipation. She hadn't bound him, rather instructing him to strip and grasp the fat links. She'd then pinched those nipples between cloverleaf clamps and connected them to the chains overhead. A particularly evil move as they would inflict pain if his chest moved more than an inch or two from his current position.

"You'll stay like this, yes?" she'd asked.

He'd acknowledged her request. Her choice was going to test him. He craved the helplessness of being bound, the utter and complete relinquishment of freedom. To him, to trust someone with his body so completely they could do anything to him, was the ultimate gift he could bestow on a Dominant. When that gift was acknowledged with a smile, a word that showed he or she was pleased, Laurent drifted into a state of pure relaxation. Steffan had watched Laurent succumb to this bliss many times. His near addiction to finding this state almost cost him his life in Amsterdam. He'd done all he could. Now with Sarah's help, he would learn a new way.

She ran her fingernails over Laurent's pecs and down his abdomen. God, he loved watching her stalk her prey—for that's what she reminded him of, a rare lynx slipping through the bars of red light with claws out to mark her target.

The first time Steffan saw Sarah, he couldn't place her age or her nationality. Her beauty was in a class of its own, augmented by an unshakeable sense of self that ran so deep in her she had to have been born with it. He, on the other hand, had scraped together bits and pieces of confidence, laying them like pieces of chain mail until he had enough to deflect even the most outrageous attacks on his ego. In other words, he'd come about his maturity and confidence the usual way. Sarah's had to have been a gift from the Gods. From the second he'd met her, he'd tacked her image on a mental wall and held up other pictures of women against hers. None of them had measured up.

She flicked the clamps with her fingernails, and Laurent hissed.

"Too much?" she asked him.

"No, Mistress," he said between gritted teeth.

"Nicer than clothespins, don't you think?" she asked him.

"Yes, Mistress." His bobbing cock authenticated his response. The pain aroused him.

She strode back to the table of instruments and chose the largest, black leather paddle. They'd used it on the redhead the night they'd topped together. She handed it to him. "Care to do the honors?"

Steffan took it without an ounce of hesitation. Laurent had a voracious appetite for impact play. He'd once flogged and whipped Laurent for two hours before Laurent gasped *yellow.*

"His dossier says he can come from spanking," she said.

Laurent reacted with a feral moan.

"Also from flogging, and serving a Mistress's needs between her legs. I've seen Laurent eat out a woman dozens of times, his hands manacled behind him so he couldn't touch himself or her with his come spurting over his belly and her legs."

When Laurent's whimper sounded like a plea, her eyes sprang to him. Her eyelids dropped, and one corner of her mouth tipped as she placed her hands on his pecs. Did the thought of him going down on her make her wet?

He circled Laurent. The man's ass clenched as if in readiness for the paddle. Steffan knew it was more likely from his desperation to come. Sarah's hands on him had to have the same impact as having his cock sucked. He'd known that sure, confident, and at times, compassionate touch of hers. Heady stuff for a Dom and impossibly arousing for a sub like

Laurent. Pre-cum leaked from the head of Laurent's visibly pulsing cock. The man was in a bad way and they'd barely gotten started. Steffan chuckled to himself darkly. He wasn't any better condition, his cock beginning to ache just from being so near to Sarah.

Tucking the paddle between his elbow and side, he unbuttoned his shirt, letting the two sides splay open, and rolled up his sleeves.

A rustle of fabric drew his attention back to Sarah. She stood in a sheer nude thong with her skirt puddled at her feet. A dark trail of wet lined the seam between her legs and damn if his cock didn't harden further. She unbuttoned that prim, white blouse—the kind that fired the imagination of fifteen-year-old boys with librarian fantasies. God, her dark raspberry nipples were easily visible through a bra made of the same sheer material as her thong. His mouth watered at the thought of how they'd taste. She stepped out of her skirt and reached down for it, not wobbling once in *those* heels.

He'd asked her to keep those shoes on while he took her from behind as she lay over his quartz bar top. That memory of being buried between her legs, enjoying her, exploding in her, surfaced so clearly as it had many times over the last two years.

Her eyes moved to Laurent whose fists clenched around links, his fingers whitening with strain. Her heels clicked against the concrete as she took careful steps toward him. She captured one of his legs between her knees and pressed her crotch into his thigh. "Feel my hot pussy, Laurent? That's what I might let you have later if you're a good boy. You did say once you wished to take care of me."

That's all the man needed to hear to go all night, if necessary.

"It would be my honor, Mistress," Laurent said, half whisper, half gasp.

She pushed off him, a smile forming on her face. She turned to him and the woman of endless surprises, surprised him once more. She winked. Steffan stood feet away from someone he desired with unprecedented strength and who turned him away repeatedly. He was here now. He'd make the best of it.

"Such a beautiful man," she said under her breath.

"Told you," Steffan said. "Falling in love. It's inevitable."

"Me? Or you?"

My, how quickly she'd entered his brain.

"We're Dominants," he said. "We want it all."

She laid a hand across Laurent's cheek and smiled into his eyes. Laurent tensed from anticipating the endorphins she'd cause, not fear of pain. Laurent flourished by proving he could endure whatever a Dom handed out—another reason Steffan trusted only her with Laurent.

For a split second, he wrestled with a thought that it was her unshakable adherence to safety that both comforted and irritated him. She shielded herself with protocol. It kept him from cracking her heart. Was that what he wanted to do? *Yes.* He wanted inside her emotions. He wanted her to lay down her defenses.? As she stood proudly in those heels, her eyes flicking to him as if waiting for his participation, how could he have deluded himself he was only here for Laurent?

Laurent groaned when she cupped his balls with her other hand. "I'm going to leave this free, Laurent. You are not to come until I say so."

"I won't."

Steffan pulled back and landed a crack across his backside.

"I won't, Mistress," he corrected.

She turned and placed her back against Laurent, capturing his cock between the small of her back and his groin. "Whenever you're ready, Steffan."

Inventive, he thought. Laurent was going to get to feel her body but not have access.

Steffan pulled back and landed another blow against Laurent's ass, pitching him into her. He hadn't used his full force. He didn't want Laurent to send her flying off her feet and into the mirror. He shouldn't have bothered to be careful for she had planted her feet wide, and Laurent would make sure his Mistress wasn't harmed. That, he knew for sure.

Laurent dropped his head so his face got closer to her hair and inhaled. When he lifted those eyelashes that women swooned over, Sarah was staring back at him in the mirror wearing a half-smile. This was going to be torture for both him and Laurent, and she knew it.

Laurent stared at him in the mirror. *Don't you dare hold back, Steffan,* his eyes relayed. That little bit of nonsense earned him a light blow, as a warning.

"Don't even think about calling the shots here," he whispered into his ear. The warning had its intended effect. Laurent lowered his eyes.

For long minutes he rained blows on Laurent. The man's hips banged against the small of her back, his cock rubbing against her with no hope of release. Laurent's grunts grew more frustrated as she pushed herself against him, her hair teasing his chest, her scent rising from the friction between their bodies.

"More," she instructed, and raised one leg, placing her heel against the mirror, giving them both a view of her pussy, glistening and wet. She expertly balanced on one leg while pushing herself against Laurent's body for leverage. He was sure Laurent was having the same reaction inside—let go, drop everything, wrap arms around her to steady her. Yet, if either did, she'd be pissed.

Sarah began to undulate against him, and Laurent's back muscles strained. His ass clenched, a strangled please on his lips evident. To be mashed against such a glorious body but not be able to touch and bound only by his self-discipline had to be excruciating for him.

Steffan paddled Laurent, hard, for an excruciating twenty minutes, not relenting until his ass was deep purple in the red light. He almost stopped when Sarah slipped her fingers into her panties. He mastered himself quickly, or fuck him, he would come in his pants from the sight in the mirror. He pulled out every trick he'd ever used to keep himself from spewing. She panted hard as she worked herself. Laurent's chest rapidly expanded and contracted. His fists clenched so hard on the chains above Steffan worried he might tear the skin.

She brought her leg down and pivoted so fast Laurent tumbled forward, a cry bursting from his lips as the nipple clamps hit the end of their chains. She removed the clamps from his nipples and left them to dangle. She leaned against the mirror and widened her stance.

"Laurent, let go of the chains and drop to your knees. Taste me."

Such direct words from the woman shook Steffan from his growing stupor as he realized her intent. Laurent had not been in such a daze, as he instantly let go and fell to his knees. He buried his face between her legs in a second. Her mouth dropped opened as he gripped her thighs and his mouth latched on to her. Wet, sucking sounds mixed with the rattle of the chains still swaying in front of him.

Sarah stared at Steffan, her eyes glazing in pleasure as Laurent took his fill. Fuck him, he should be causing that reaction. He should be triggering that flush across her chest, her cheeks. He stalked forward, placing both hands on either side of her face, widening his legs so Laurent could continue his work below him. The rise in her chin, the challenge that filled her eyes, didn't make him falter one bit. She turned him on. Not because he had an interest in being on the receiving end of her domination, but because she was so clearly unfettered in her power—something he'd always admired about women.

He leaned in, fisting her hair and took her mouth. She opened to him. He savaged her lips, driven by greed and the need to claim, and she responded with equal ferocity. His groin ached from lack of contact as she met him with every bit of her power, dueling with him in something as simple as a kiss.

Her hands yanked at his belt. When those soft hands met his cock, he moaned into her mouth. She drew him out, gentler than he expected given her assault on his trousers, and stroked. Her touches, her mouth, the wet sucking sounds below him, would drive any sane man mad. He had to have this woman underneath him.

He released her mouth, both of them panting.

"Come for me," she said.

"Not unless it's inside you," he told her. "Laurent, you heard your Mistress."

She pulled her hand free from him, and he heard Laurent's guttural release below him. Only one of them took orders. It wasn't him.

He stepped backward and tucked himself into his pants. Laurent had sagged against her thighs, breathing heavily but not pulling back. She expertly slipped herself from both men. Laurent's haunted eyes darted up to Steffan. Wet glistened on his jaw.

After retrieving a towel, she crouched down to Laurent. He placed his hands on the towel before she could make a move to clean him up.

"Mistress, may I please—"

She placed a finger against his lips. "You did so well.

Exactly what I wanted." She then placed a kiss on his forehead.

"But—"

"Hush. Take the gifts I give you." Her voice was steel.

As she went to work cleaning him up, Laurent's eyes flashed to him with a question. Sarah hadn't orgasmed. Why did she deny herself?

## 21

He arrived at Sarah's for work the next day, as promised. They didn't speak about last night, and it had nothing to do with the fact that Madeline, Sarah's assistant, was present. He didn't know what to say—or ask. For now, he'd listen and look for the opening to talk to Sarah when alone.

They'd stayed in the dungeon together for a grand total of ten more minutes after she denied him the pleasure of bringing her to orgasm. Sarah had gotten dressed. He'd gone to the bathroom off the dungeon to clean up, insisting he go alone. He'd meant to give Steffan and Sarah a chance to talk. It was the wrong thing to do, as he'd returned to find them snapping at one another.

"This is all I can offer, Steffan. It really should be enough," she'd hissed in a whisper.

Steffan had turned to him, lips drawn tight. "Ready to go?"

Sarah had hugged him, held his face and asked if he was all right. He'd been fine, god-damn-it. It was Sarah who hadn't been fine. She asked him to come to work today, which he had done. Hell, he'd have done anything she asked

—anything except dance around what had happened. Or, not happened. The three of them had played, and it had been glorious. She'd denied herself, which was her right, and Steffan just had to press her about it. He was so angry at Steffan, he'd barely spoken to the man.

He'd spent a silent morning helping Sarah fit Jonathan for his wedding tuxedo—or tried to. Sarah's mother's constant stream of commentary considerably slowed down things.

The instant Laurent had arrived, Claire Marillioux strode up to him in that horrid peach suit that had to be vintage Chanel, and introduced herself to him immediately. "I'm Sarah's mother, Claire." Her bleached hair had been processed so much it resembled blond cotton candy. Her eyebrows were penciled in hard. Paper-thin skin and cool pieces of metal met his hand in her handshake. She sported so many diamonds on her hands, he worried about Jonathan's sleeve getting snagged, given she couldn't stop picking off imaginary lint. Laurent had brushed the coats just that morning.

"How women do this all day, I will never know." Jonathan straightened his suit coat sleeves and stepped off the platform in the fitting room.

"Oh, Jonathan, we don't." Sarah's mother said. "Women don't require as many fittings as men. We know our measurements by heart."

"My mother," Sarah laughed. "She was born knowing if her thighs grew 1000th of an inch."

Laurent didn't doubt it.

"Laurent, why aren't you one of Sarah's models?" Claire smiled at him. She and Sarah had similar mouths, though Claire's lift of the lips never reached her eyes, probably to avoid creating wrinkles in her new eye job—or at least Laurent guessed it was new by the tightly drawn skin. He normally didn't think such uncharitable thoughts, but his insides were strung too tight over last night.

"Thank you, Mrs. Brond, but I prefer to help Sarah in other ways."

"Where did you two meet again?" she asked, though he'd certainly not said where a first time.

"Through a mutual friend."

"Oh really? How fascinating." She turned to Sarah who was already saying her good-byes to Jonathan. "Jonathan? Are you done already? You seem as eager to leave this place as your fiancé."

His face hardened. "It's hard to enjoy things when the details start to overrun the purpose. We won't be doing this again, Claire. Dress fittings and changes are done." He spun on his heel and exited.

"You young people and your work," she said. "There is so much else to life, wouldn't you agree, Laurent?"

"I would agree completely, Mrs. Brond. It's important to know how to let off steam." He was pressing things, but why not? Steffan had his way of pushing, but Laurent had his own way of forcing an issue. He gathered a pair of trousers, abandoned by Jonathan.

"My God, Sarah. The man picks up clothes from the floor. Marry him." Claire laughed.

Laurent gave Sarah a smile that she did not return.

Alexander stepped through the fitting room door and in a few short strides was centered on the dais.

"Alexander, I do believe you could bring back the three-piece suit," Claire circled him on the podium. "What do you think, Laurent?"

"I agree completely." The man could bring the Nehru jacket back in style.

Alexander unbuttoned his jacket. "There was a time when men didn't leave the house without one on."

"Nice," Laurent let slip out.

"Alexander, the fit is perfect," Sarah said.

"Agreed." He stepped off the podium.

"People move fast in this city, Laurent. Too fast if you ask me," Claire scowled

"I'm seeing you at Charlotte's event, right?" Sarah took the jacket Alexander shrugged off.

Laurent's gaze shot up at the mention of Charlotte and her collaring ceremony, the "event" subterfuge necessary given the number of people in the room who were not associated with Accendos.

"I wouldn't miss it."

"Who's Charlotte?" Claire asked.

"A friend."

"Well, I'm glad you're getting out. Really, Laurent, all my daughter does is work. Perhaps you could change that."

"I would love to change that."

Sarah inspected Alexander's cuffs, likely to make sure they fell at the exact point she desired. Her attention to detail rivaled Steffan's attention to his cooking, which he seemed to be doing less of. He'd cooked the other night and baked a few pastries here and there, yet their kitchen counters remained wide open, appliances still boxed, and that gorgeous quartz-topped island was littered with too many take-out menus.

"Hmm, we need the other cufflinks," she said. "I'll be right back."

Laurent jumped on the chance to follow her out—alone. As soon as the curtains closed behind him, she spun. "Laurent, what?"

"I'm worried about you. Even your mother—"

"The dynamic in our family has been long established."

Sadness crossed her face, but then she recovered. She

swiped the curtain back and stepped back into the store-room. Okay, that didn't go as planned. He followed.

"Sarah, dear," her mother began. "The new suits are divine. It is the eleventh hour to change things, but—"

"We can't, mother," Sarah said. "No more changes. It's done."

She sighed dramatically and looked over at Laurent. "You'll find my daughter is quite the stickler for schedules and such."

"I appreciate that."

"Ask her out anyway, if you haven't already."

The icicles Sarah aimed at her mother impaled his heart.

Alexander stepped forward. "Sarah, I'd like to see if my suit for that other event came in?"

Sarah straightened. "Of course, Alexander. I completely forgot. Mother, you will be late for your lunch unless you hurry."

"Yes, I probably will be." She also looked sad.

Why did no one get what they wanted in this town?

Sarah pulled out Alexander's new black kilt and turned to find her mother had *not* left, but rather followed her into the storeroom.

"I just need a smidgen of your time, daughter of mine." She turned and yanked the curtains closer together. This was not going to be good.

She strode over to Sarah. "Now, you don't ever like hearing this from me—"

"We are not changing another detail of this wedding, Mother."

Claire wrinkled her forehead. "I'm talking about *Laurent.*

Now there is a man you could get used to. He is quite smitten with you."

"Smitten?" Sarah laughed.

"What's he going to school for? Fashion? Law school?"

"Physical therapy. Mother, we are not doing this."

"Like I said." She raised her hands. "You never want to hear this from me, but my God, Sarah, you attract men like flies. That one out there can't keep his eyes off you. Why won't you let go for once?"

"Stop."

Claire nearly stepped backward at her tone—one Sarah normally used on bratty submissives. Before she could turn away, her mother grasped her arm with surprising strength. "Sarah. Please. I love you."

That did stop her in her tracks.

"Mother, are you crying?" Yes, those were honest to god tears in her eyes.

"I know this wedding hasn't been easy on anyone. I want my children to be happy, and I know how regrets can take over your life—like you're doing now."

"I don't know what—"

"It won't happen again. I can assure you." Her mother then did the inexplicable. She moved closer and took both her hands. Her voice in her throat. Affection wasn't Claire's strong suit.

"Joshua Martin," Claire said. "There. I said his name out loud. It's time we finally did."

Sarah couldn't breathe, but God help her if she fainted, she'd kill herself. No, first she'd kill her mother.

The curtains parted, and Alexander strode in. "Claire, tell me you didn't just say what I thought I heard."

So he'd overheard. He was one of the few people in the world who knew that name and knew what it would do to her to hear it spoken aloud. There wasn't anything he could do, however, to lessen the impact of hearing the boy's name she'd nearly been ruined over. There wasn't anything anyone could do.

Laurent's arms were full of men's jackets, still warm from being worn. He couldn't help but sneak a peek inside the storeroom. Alexander's face was as hard as his voice. So what, Laurent eavesdropped. He wasn't sorry. He had to find out what was going on in Sarah's head. Instead, he caught a name that drained all the color from Sarah's face. *Joshua Martin?* Who was Joshua Martin?

A second later, Sarah had rushed through the curtains without giving him a single look as she brushed passed. She'd gone straight to her office, the door clicking behind her.

Alexander's voice thundered through the curtain. "Claire, I'm appalled you would mention that name."

"She's my daughter. I have an idea how—"

"She doesn't need your ideas, Claire. She needs your love."

Alexander swiped the curtain back, and Laurent stepped backward. He dipped his head. Alexander had just caught him snooping. He couldn't look at the man.

"Laurent." Alexander stepped out and allowed a flustered Claire to slip by him. The woman picked up her purse and looked back at Alexander.

"It's time, Alexander," she said.

"I know." His voice had softened.

"Then do something. Please. You're her closest friend." Claire swallowed hard.

Laurent, too afraid to look at Alexander, believed the man gave her some sort of signal because she smiled and nodded before she moved across the room and out the exit.

A heavy hand fell on his shoulder. "Laurent, you overheard that."

"Who's Joshua Martin?" He pried.

"Someone from Sarah's past. You'd be wise never to bring it up with her."

"He hurt her."

"Yes."

"What can I do? I love her." There, he'd said it aloud.

Alexander eyed him. "Some people in our world keep looking for their soul mate, the one who will answer all your dreams. Some find that. Take Jonathan and Christiana, for example. As for Sarah?"

"She found the one and lost him."

"No, quite the opposite."

"I don't understand."

"Not my story to tell. But she was devastated."

"So, now she won't let anyone do that to her again?"

"You're quite perceptive, Laurent. But, not exactly. You want to know the key to Sarah? Give her more choices, not fewer."

"More."

"I think you know what I mean. Not everyone wants to be like a swan—tied to one person the rest of their lives." The man took the armful of suits Laurent held, now wrinkled to oblivion, in his arms. Alexander hung them on hooks, one-by-one. "So many choices." He stepped back and looked at the army of jackets. "Why should anyone have to choose just one?"

"I agree."

After Alexander left, Laurent stood deep in thought for long moments. Finally, he pursed his lips and shrugged. "Why not? It should work." He slipped outside to the parking lot, now dim in twilight, and pulled out his phone.

"Steffan. I know what to do."

There was a moment of silence on the other end, but Laurent didn't need to say "I know what to do with Sarah" for he doubted his friend could think of anyone else right now. He certainly couldn't.

"I'm listening," Steffan said.

Laurent told him about his mysterious, though enlightening, conversation with Alexander, and offered up a plan—one that would involve both of them. Choices, the man had said. Okay, they would give her just that.

## 22

Sarah stepped through the massive Gothic oak door of The Library into a fairy wonderland. They'd had to move Charlotte's collaring ceremony inside due to rain, but the girl still got what she wanted.

Tiny white lights hung in long drapes across the entire ceiling, creating a lower ceiling than normally existed. Through the lighted strands, she noted swags of white flowers hung on all the balconies of the upper decks—roses, gardenias, baby's breath and more. The Library, normally dark and heavy, seemed bathed in moonlight. "So like Charlotte," she said under her breath without an ounce of cynicism.

"Sarah, I thought you were on vacation?" Carson strode over and pecked her on the cheek.

"No, just work."

"Wedding crunch time? You know there is a reason why London and I eloped."

She laughed. "I can think of a hundred reasons why you'd want to now. But Jonathan ..."

"The romantic pussy," Carson said.

She laughed heartily for the first time in days. She'd forgotten how good it felt to be among friends. She had hidden away for the last few days and tried to catch up on sleep. How could anyone sleep after her mother dropped an explosive name from her past like it was nothing? Like it wouldn't send her reeling from the memories evoked? She couldn't bear to think of Joshua Martin and the string of broken hearts—including her own—he'd left. Now she was among her chosen family, and she needed to think of more important things like her friends.

"Where is London?" she asked.

"Ladies room with Christiana and the pack."

Carson called all the significant others of the Tribunal Council members, "the pack." She supposed it was apropos given how they looked after one another, protected one another, and that included her. She'd remember that the next time her she was within a mile of the woman who'd given birth to her but clearly didn't understand the definition of protection.

Carson studied her. "How are you really, Sarah? You look tired."

"Insomnia, and, the melatonin I took gave me bad dreams."

"Well, remember about the candle that burned both ends."

"It made a sub very happy?" a female chirp asserted from behind her.

"Exactly. Hello, wife," Carson placed a kiss on London's temple as the woman sidled up to him.

"Hi, Sarah, love your shoes."

"Giuseppe Zapotti." She cocked her ankle, showing off the Swarovski crystal hearts along the copper-colored straps. "Come by. I have a pair for you."

"Oh, you don't need—"

"Oh, yes, she does," Carson said. "They will look stunning

on you. Thanks, Sarah. Always taking care of others." He winked at her, and her eyes pricked.

Jesus, she was emotional today. Seemed they all were by the way Carson's face softened—and the man never softened.

"Look at the two of us," he said. "Getting all emotional over shoes."

"Well, they are Zapotti's. Plus, look at where we are." London raised her gaze to the fairy lights.

"Agreed." Sarah downed her champagne and grabbed another from a passing tray carried by a wait staff member she didn't recognize. Not like her to day-drink, but you know what? *Fuck it.* She wasn't someone to swear, but it felt good to say that in her mind.

A Scottish bagpipe sounded, startling several of the two dozen guests. The piper paraded through the main doors, adopting the traditional gliding slow-step, the tassels on his sporran swinging, the nasal whine of the pipes blotting out any remnants of conversation. Behind him, Alexander walked in time. His black Argyle jacket atop a black kilt set off his salt and pepper hair and closely trimmed beard. Two male attendants closed the doors behind them.

The crowd parted, allowing the two men to stride up to Master R, also striking in an all-black suit, who stood on a large square of white cloth. He watched the now-closed doors with such intention, she peeped backward herself.

Alexander stopped next to Richard and began to speak.

"Welcome friends. And, welcome, Charlotte Braden."

All eyes turned to The Library doors. Tony and Amos each grasped a handle and opened the door wide to reveal Charlotte. Her yellow gossamer dress billowed and strands of her red hair, left loose and curled, rose up in the sudden shift of air. She stood between Marcos and Isabella Santos, both in black. The escorts symbolized Master and submissive—both sides of a coin that no one in this room misspent.

Sarah's heart swelled with pride at her friends. Marcos had been a friend of Charlotte's late husband and had stepped in to take care of her after her husband died. It wasn't a surprise. Shrugging off conventional social norms, her close circle followed their hearts, never leaving one of their own bereft and unfulfilled, stepping in when needed.

Her eyes threatened tears as Charlotte's two escorts led her into the room, her pale yellow sharp against so much black. There was no hesitation in her movements, no fear in those eyes. Charlotte had come far, overcome so much. Suddenly, Sarah felt burdened by the passage of time— how much had changed for others and had not changed for her. She forced her shoulders back, her spine to straighten. This was a happy day, not a time to reflect on the past.

Charlotte proceeded slowly up the make-shift aisle. The other faces blurred into the background, except for a pair of blue eyes from across the room. Steffan nodded at her once. Laurent, in the Tiger of Sweden jacket she'd gifted him, knelt by his side. She inhaled sharply, as if she'd been holding her breath, and shook off her moment of paralysis.

She quickly glanced away, Charlotte once again the determined sole focus of her attention.

After reaching Richard, Marcos placed Charlotte's hand on his arm, then gave him a mock punch in the arm. Richard didn't notice the gesture, as his eyes locked on the woman before him.

The bagpipe stopped abruptly, and the piper retreated to stand, chin raised, in the corner.

"Friends," Alexander's voice boomed. "We are gathered here today to witness a collaring, a joining of two souls, a Master and slave, who wish to celebrate their committed relationship to one another. Master R, Richard Randall and Charlotte Braden. Richard will express that commitment by offering this collar to Charlotte to be worn evermore so long as they live."

He held up a glittering choker which Sarah immediately recognized as real diamonds. She wouldn't have expected anything less from Richard. The man hadn't managed to take his eyes off Charlotte yet.

"Submissives, you will stand for this ceremony," Alexander said. "Your witnessing of these events is vital, for you are the blood in our hearts, the energy in our bones, the love in our souls."

She sensed movement, people standing. She'd let her eyes go soft, fuzzy, trying not to take in the details of anyone too closely, rather absorbing herself in the energy around her. She refused to look at Steffan and Laurent during this ceremony.

"Dominants, your witnessing of these events today also is vital," he continued. "You are the structure, the control, the direction. You are the North Star. Together, Top and bottom, Dominant and submissive, Master and slave, we balance our world—together. One does not exist without the other."

Against her will, her eyes found Steffan's again. He had continued to stare directly at her—confident but not at all filled with the ice she'd seen so often. Perhaps the ceremony was impacting him as well.

"A collar is more than this metal I hold," Alexander's words rang through the large space.

"Or diamonds," she whispered.

Steffan nodded as if he'd heard her or least read her lips. His features had blurred, and she had to blink to clear her vision. If no one was in this room, she believed she could lie down on this carpet and fall asleep. Even breathing seemed to take effort.

Alexander's words rose and fell, nearly hypnotic in their effect. "It is a symbol of how deeply they cherish, respect and serve one another. This is a sacred joining. Do you, my friends, support this union and promise to help provide whatever they need to fulfill these destinies as they have so chosen?"

"We do." The mix of male and female voices joined and rang around her. Steffan's lips had formed the words, but all she could feel was the slide of his mouth over hers as it had in that red light in the dungeon, her back pressed into the cold mirror.

Charlotte now knelt before her Master. He took the collar from a small pillow, but when she lifted that curtain of red hair, he simply placed it around her neck. He didn't fasten it. He knelt down so they were face-to-face and tipped up her chin so she would look directly into his eyes. He whispered so low his words blurred into a deep male murmur. A smile spread across her delicate features, and a single word crossed her lips. *Forever.* He then ran his fingertips around her neck, and the click of the collar rang in Sarah's mind as loud as any church bell.

A drop of moisture fell on her hand. She swiped her cheek and came away with wet. The event deserved her emotion. She *should* be touched by the beauty of what she witnessed. Charlotte and Richard were a couple who were meant to be together. *Together.* Such an interesting word. If broken apart it read *to get her.* That's what Joshua had wanted. He had wanted Sarah to the point where he'd sacrificed everything for her, and then he'd died.

Laurent was embracing Charlotte. Steffan was congratulating Richard. The ceremony had ended while she'd been lost in her own regrets. Steffan and Laurent backed away, and let others give their congratulations to the couple, now hand-in-hand. By the look of his Master R's grip, he might never let go. Once the crowd swallowed Steffan and Laurent, she strode over to Master R.

"Congratulations." She gave him a kiss on the cheek and then caught the emotion in his eyes. She agreed with the male pride that shone there for he'd also been chosen by Charlotte.

"Thank you, Sarah. For everything," Charlotte threw her arms around her.

"It was so beautiful. You are beautiful."

Charlotte let go and then clasped her hands. "It's what you do."

Before she could ask what the girl meant, Charlotte was swallowed up by more well-wishers. Sarah backed up, and a wave of fatigue swamped her so completely she could barely keep her eyes open. She'd give anything to lie down for just a few minutes. Perhaps she'd slip upstairs and take a power nap. No one would notice, and no one would come looking for her.

## 23

Steffan felt Sarah's absence the second she left the room. The energy flattened, the light dimmed. He'd been stopped by Ryan, congratulating him on his recent admittance to Accendos. Laurent was across the room talking to Carrie. His eyes darted in his direction. Ah, so he'd noticed she was gone, as well. He would. The man was in love with Sarah. Well, shit, so was he.

He didn't lie to himself. Why would he? Yes, he was in love with a woman who was irritatingly stingy with herself, gracious and giving to others—everyone but him. It made him wonder what the hell was going on. He was going to find out.

During the ceremony, he hadn't been about to take his eyes off her. The weariness she wore like those strappy sandals no match for her beauty. They had to hurt, but he understood how someone could get used to pain until it became part of the background noise. So she'd been hurt by someone? Join the club. It was time for them to form their own club, of sorts.

He and Laurent had talked—more words passed between

them over the last two days than they'd spoken to each other in the last two years combined. They'd admitted where they stood and agreed on one thing. It wasn't going to be an either-or situation where they were concerned. She'd get both of them—if she chose them. It was now their sole mission to force that choice.

After a few pleasantries, Steffan made his excuses to Ryan without apology.

He looked down the hallway to see her standing before the elevator. He and Laurent got to it just in time to see her jog down the steps, out the French doors to the garden, and into the pouring rain.

"She did not …" Laurent said to the glass. "She's wearing a vintage Diane Von Furstenberg …"

Steffan was out the door in less time than it took Laurent to finish his sentence. Hard pelts of rain soaked him to the bone before reaching the fountain. The sky had darkened with thunderclouds giving the late afternoon sky the look of twilight. A boom overhead silenced the tell-tale click of heels against wet stones. She'd kill herself running in those sandals.

After frantically searching down one path, he finally found her under the thick canopy of a tree, water streaming down her cheeks, tendrils of hair plastered to the side of her face. Sopping wet, she was still more glamorous than any woman he'd never laid eyes on.

"You want to tell me what you're doing?" He pointed to her dress. "Laurent tells me that's vintage."

She chuffed. "You should be worried about ruining your own suit."

"I'm worried about you." He ducked under the tree boughs to stand before her. At least the placement sheltered them from the hardest rain.

"Don't be," she said.

"I'd say anyone who runs across wet flagstones in those heels—"

"Death heels."

"Even worse."

"I'm fine, Steffan."

"No, you're not." He raised his hand to stop her protest. "Sometimes the woman who takes care of everyone needs someone to be there for her."

"You're going to miss the party."

"I'm not going to *miss* anything." He stepped forward and took her face in his hands.

She didn't reply, but her eyes held such sadness something broke inside him.

"I'm sorry," he said because a man who couldn't apologize wasn't a man. "I'm sorry I let so much time pass after London. I'm sorry that I backed away the other night. And, by the way, that's over."

"Which part?"

"All of it."

She grew so still, he could have mistaken her for the statue of Venus that stood feet away.

"Now I'm going to kiss you. Going to stop me?"

"No."

He took her mouth and knew she would be the last woman he'd ever kiss in his lifetime.

# 24

Steffan pulled her closer just as she sensed herself slipping. He turned her so he leaned against the tree and she was pressed into him, held up by his arms. God, she was tired, the kind of exhaustion that seeps into your bones. She didn't know why she'd turned to the garden instead of going to her room. Maybe because the gardens had always brought her answers. Maybe because she was going crazy.

The patter of raindrops on leaves, the taste of his mouth now kissing her, the warmth of his skin seeping through his thin shirt—she clung to each sense. She let him kiss her. She was clear on that. She didn't feel taken, rather appreciated. He was kissing the woman, not just the Dominant like he had so many years ago.

Steffan could make it so easy for her to forget all the reasons she kept herself from falling in love. Maybe it was what she'd just witnessed—such beauty between two people as they declared before the world they belonged to one another. *Belonging*. Isn't that what Steffan had said Laurent wanted?

She panted into his mouth now, his cock hardening

between her legs. She rubbed up against him, ground herself shamelessly, feeling his length, remembering how he filled her, how time had suspended that weekend. She could use some of that now. She'd grown brittle in recent years. *Aloof.* It was safer for her, but safer for all around her, too. She had no idea how to reverse that course—and she had no desire to.

A hand, not Steffan's, fell onto her back. Another man's body pressed into her from behind. "I'm here, Mistress." Laurent's soft voice soothed that last, tense, part of her.

She tilted her pelvis forward and then backward, teasing each cock pressed into her—Steffan's between her legs, as he slouched slightly to even their height difference, and Laurent's who nestled just above the base of her spine. God, she did love men—their hardness, their unexpected soft places, the stubborn focus.

Steffan broke his kiss. His glacial blue eyes fixed on her face in question.

"Better," she said and reached back to cradle the back of Laurent's head with one hand. She bowed backward, and Steffan took the opportunity to place his lips to her neck. Power surged through her as these two men touched her, grew hard because of her.

"What may I do for you, Mistress?" Laurent whispered, ever the submissive who wishes permission at every turn.

"Take me to my room." When she lifted her head, that glacial blue in Steffan's eyes turned to a dark storm.

He dropped his arms and let her right herself. She hooked her arm into Laurent's and held the other hand out to Steffan in invitation. He took it, and they walked, joined, to her room, past guests, guards, and assistants, and she didn't care.

As soon as her bedroom door clicked shut, Steffan twirled her around, but this time, she rose up and took possession of his mouth. His hands dove under her dress and found her ass. He hiked her up so she got yet another connection with his cock trapped inside his ruined trousers. She wrestled with his jacket until together they managed to get him out of it.

Rushing water—not too far and not too close—signaled her shower had been turned on.

"We need to warm you up," Steffan said and led her to the bathroom. Laurent stood by the shower door, fully nude, his cock beckoning her forward. She wanted to taste him. Before the night was over, she would.

Ripping sounded behind her, as Steffan shed himself of his clothes.

"Mistress, may I?" Laurent touched the tie around her wrap dress.

"You may." The fabric stubbornly stuck to her skin, but together they managed to get her dress, panties, and bra off.

The three of them stepped into the shower, all four shower heads hitting their skin, caressing their muscles, with blessedly hot water. Laurent kneaded her shoulders, while Steffan resumed his welcomed assault on her mouth. The man could kiss. Her bare breasts rubbed up against his firm chest, while Laurent's cock pressed into the small of her back. When all the fatigue had been worked out by Laurent's magic fingers, she broke herself free from both of them.

Taking a wide stance, she leaned into the corner of the shower. She stood there for a glorious second, feeling every bit of her femaleness. She trailed her hand up her belly to the underside of her left breast and circled her nipple with her fingertip.

Laurent swallowed, while Steffan's eyes grew fierce, the blue filling with a dark lust. She'd always known her power over men like she'd told them at that dinner—though she'd made sure to use it more wisely in her later years than when she was young. Tonight, she was going to let it all go—the past and the future—and just ... feel.

"Laurent. Taste me."

He dropped to his knees and buried his face, his tongue finding her center. She kept her eyes on Steffan as Laurent trailed his hot tongue between her inner folds, up one side and down the other. Steffan reached for himself and stroked, that slightly haughty tilt of his chin never dipping as his friend serviced her. Laurent flicked her clit and made her gasp. He lapped up the sides, only to return to nip and suck on her most sensitive part.

"You've got a wicked tongue, Laurent," she breathed into the steam. As his mouth did its dance on her pussy, Stefan continued to stroke himself, a lazy smile on his face contradicting his tense jaw.

"I want inside you," Steffan said.

She wanted that, too, but didn't respond. Instead, her breath now came in rapid gulps as Laurent ate her, hard and greedily. She grasped the back of his head, her fingers threading through dark curls, as she pressed him harder against her. She then did what she'd wanted to the other night, but hadn't. She closed her eyes and shattered against his mouth. When she came back to herself, she raised her lids and found Steffan.

"I didn't think it was possible for you to be more beautiful than you are." Steffan stroked harder, the purple head of his cock, swollen and shiny. "But, right then, watching you come undone? A goddess. Tonight, I am going to see more of that pleasure on your face."

Once she let go of his head, Laurent eased back and scooted backward as if making room for Steffan.

"Yes," she said. A simple word, but all he needed to break through the water spray to reach for her. He hitched her up against the warming tiles. She wrapped her legs around him, and he drove forward, finding what he wanted. God, that first thrust filled and stretched her to the maximum. Her pussy registered every millimeter of his cock, the head so close to her cervix a dull ache began. "I want more."

He waited for her to adjust, but only for a few seconds before he began to fuck her, his hands cushioning the small of her back. Slaps of flesh echoed against the tiles. She loved that he was getting off on her as much as she was on him. There was such beauty in the give and take of it all. Alexander had always said, " Ying and yang was made for people like us." *Us.*

Her second orgasm came quickly on the heels of the first, this one smaller but deeper, sparked by that thick length pushing and pulling on her insides. She hadn't let another man inside her this way in two years—not since Steffan, and now she knew why. Why be disappointed when she knew they wouldn't compare? They might understand her need for dominance, but to be with someone who could give her pleasure and *not* be submitting to her, but instead *matching* her, was as rare as a miracle.

Steffan roared into her neck, finding his own release, not requiring her permission. Steffan hadn't once tried to top her two years ago, yet he hadn't backed down. They'd worked in concert, pleasing each other, enjoying one another, just as they were doing now.

He eased her legs down and pulled her forward into a kiss.

The three found themselves in her bed, still damp from the shower, bodies moving slickly over one another once more.

Sarah, between them, had her arms around Laurent, her breasts pushed into his shoulder blades. She stroked his cock.

"Hold off for me, yes?" She nipped his ear.

"Yes, Mistress."

Behind her, Steffan blew a long breath across her neck as he seated his cock inside her again. Despite being on their sides, it was a dominating position, which she balanced by teasing Laurent with slight strokes on his erection. Steffan gripped her hips and yanked her backward, dragging her over his hard length.

"Laurent, turn around." She released his cock, and he did what she asked. She hitched a leg over his and offered him a breast, which he sucked into his hot mouth. His cock nestled against her belly as he laved one nipple and then moved to the next. She buried her face in all that glorious hair. She inhaled his scent and felt the stretch of Steffan inside her. His lips were on her neck, Laurent's lips on her breast. *Drag and push.* Steffan's cock moved in and out.

She continued to play her fingers lightly over Laurent back until a choked sound came from his throat to accompany the grunts of pleasure as Steffan maintained a rhythmic thrusting.

"Please ..." The words formed around her breast as his lips hadn't left her flesh, his pelvis pitching forward seeking relief. She clucked, and only when his hips stilled did she reach for him. He scooted up so she could grasp a hold of his cock.

"You'd like to come, wouldn't you, Laurent?"

A frantic longing filled his eyes making him look wild and unrestrained.

"I want to feel you in my hand," she said. "But keep sucking on me. It pleases me."

He had drawn up to his knees to keep his cock in her hand and to reach her breast. He managed it. He flicked her nipple, first one and then moving to the other, over and over until she'd hardened into steel points.

She dragged her top leg higher and opened herself more to Steffan. Steffan's fingers drifted over her ass and under her leg. He found her clit. Let him please me, she thought. Let both of them take care of her needs, one wishing to serve, the other wishing to ... what? Did it matter?

With one arm tucked under her head, she leisurely stroked Laurent's cock, her hands moving up to the engorged head and pulling slightly on the way down. "You'd like to be inside me, wouldn't you, Laurent? Inside your Mistress?"

He nodded and sucked hard, drawing in her areola, his tongue flicking and circling her nipple, his teeth grazing ... *Oh, God.* Her head fell back. Steffan's rough five o'clock shadow brushed along her neck, her cheek. Picking up his rhythm, Steffan drove inside, pulled out and slammed back into her. His fingers now plucked her clit like a violin.

While he and Laurent weren't lovers, it seemed her words to Laurent—*you'd like to be inside me, wouldn't you?*—drove Steffan forward, to perhaps claim her? He could try all night, but she'd simply take the pleasure, the scents, the sounds all around her, and enjoy. Her fingers picked up the pace on Laurent's cock as well, and soon, under Steffan's talented hand she neared the point of cresting.

"Come for me, sweet Laurent, and let me hear you." But she only heard herself cry out as wet creamed over her hand and wrist. Steffan's his hips ground against her ass hard, a tell-tale pulse inside her that said, while the three of them hadn't come together, they'd been close.

She drifted, aware of Steffan slipping from her and Laurent's warmth drawing closer. Words were said, but she let them drift over her and then up to the sky.

She opened her eyes to find Steffan propped up on one elbow looking down at her. He tapped her nose.

"Sleep," he said.

And she did ... finally.

## 25

Her eyes cracked open, blinked at the stripe of sun that streamed across the carpet and ran over her chest. She rolled over—or tried to, as a male body instantly stopped her.

"Morning." Laurent was up on one elbow, peering down at her. His curls were tossed in random directions. He still looked like a Grecian God.

"Good Morning." Good, indeed. She'd slept last night—pressed between two warm males—for how long?

"What time is it?" she asked.

Steffan stirred, turned over, his arm pinning her to the mattress. "Afternoon," he said into her back.

"It's 1:00 p.m. You were out last night." Laurent grinned. "And this morning."

She had been asleep for 16 hours? That couldn't be. What time had they finally fallen asleep? Who cared? She felt good. *Better than good. Great.*

"I guess I needed it."

"You did." Steffan kissed between her shoulder blades, and she felt his cock pressing between her thighs.

"Mmmm, morning sex in the afternoon," he said.

"You're insatiable."

"You're a goddess." Laurent tucked a strand of hair behind her ear.

"True," she said and managed to shimmy free and slide over Laurent's body. It was time to get up, or they never would. His hands dragged over her hips as if to help her, though she noticed he held on longer than he should have. She stepped on a man's shirt on her way to the bathroom. She gathered it up.

"Didn't I teach you better than this? This is Armani." She slung it over her shoulder and marched to the bathroom. She shut the door.

She needed a moment of privacy. Her muscles complained as she did her business. She'd not had that much activity followed by that much inactivity in … ever. After brushing her teeth, she pulled her hair—a total mess since they'd all moved to the bed without drying any part of them —into a messier ponytail. Last night replayed in her brain. Okay, she'd slept with two men—one submissive, one Dominant. The submissive accepted her being in control. The Dominant? Well, he wasn't controll*able*, but it had been okay. *Oh, who are you kidding?* It had been spectacular. At some point in the evening, she'd dissolved into pure feeling, pure instinct, and let them have her. Afterward, she took them, their roles staying defined but blending like a painting. If she could have that all her life …

"Put it into perspective," she said to her reflection. One good evening did not a life make. They were here for a year. They could explore, enjoy one another. She could take this year as a vacation, of sorts. *Vacation.* She liked the sound of that.

"Oh, my god. The plane leaves first thing in the morning." She threw on the men's shirt balled up on the counter.

She slung open the door to find a smiling Steffan standing there, Laurent hovering behind him.

"I have to pack." She pushed past him.

"Freaking out?" Steffan asked.

"I don't freak out. The plane for St. Thomas leaves at 6 a.m. tomorrow morning."

"So?"

"I'll get coffee," Laurent offered.

"Perfect idea," she said. "There's a coffee cart downstairs in the bar area. Do you know where that is?"

"I do." He grabbed his pants.

"You don't need those," Steffan began.

"Oh, yes, he does," she said. "You don't want anyone to get any ideas, do you?"

Steffan chuckled and stepped aside for Laurent who stuffed his leg into his still damp and wrinkled-beyond-repair pants.

"I'll pick up some dry clothes for us, too, Steffan. Our locker," he explained.

"Great idea. Though I wouldn't mind spending a few days in here." Steffan eyeballed the bed and smiled. He stood there, tall and nude, not the least bit self-conscious. But then looking like that, why would he? A small pang between her thighs agreed.

She went to her closet, threw off the Armani shirt, and yanked on a robe before the other parts of her body took over.

As soon as Laurent left the room, Steffan moved to her. "Okay, what's wrong? It's just me."

"Why do you think something's wrong? We had a glorious night together."

"That." He pointed at her face. "That right there is what's wrong. What is with this glorious night bullshit?"

"Disappointed in last night?"

"Not in the least. In fact …" He pulled her into him.

"Like, I said, insatiable. You two are coming, right?" she asked. "To Alexander's party?"

"Hmm, if reliving last night is on the auction block? Sold."

She placed her hands on his pecs and looked up at him. "Good. Now I have things to do, like figure out what I'm wearing for five days in the heat and humidity."

He ran a finger over that soft spot over her clavicle bone, and an involuntary shudder threatened her ability to say 'no.' She had dry cleaning to retrieve, messages to return, luggage to inspect.

"What's going on in that beautiful head?" he asked.

"I can't remember where I put my bathing suit."

"Wear nothing. It's your best look." If he didn't stop that infuriating caressing …

"I'd say it's yours, too." She held out her hand to stop him from advancing on her. "Okay, let a girl do what she's gotta do." She stilled. "What?"

"I've never heard you refer to yourself as a girl before, but it fits, and take that in the best way possible, Sarah Marillioux," he admonished.

She laughed lightly. "I will if you find Laurent and make him hurry back with that coffee." She turned him and pushed him toward the door. "Then go home and pack. You will need your passport. The plane leaves from Entry Point One at 6 a.m. for Regal. We can't be late."

"Am I supposed to know what Entry Point One means?"

"No, I'll have a car pick you and Laurent up at 4 a.m. It's Alexander's party, and you know what a stickler he is for getting what he wants."

"So are you apparently. I'll book the car." He pressed a kiss to her forehead. "So, where do Laurent and I show up later? Here or at your home?"

"My home." My, how quickly she said that. Well, it made

sense for the car to pick all three of them up from one address. So they'd have another night together—not a hardship. "I'll text the address."

"I already have it." He shrugged. "Hey, no pout, you had mine, plus my entire history in that Accendos folder."

She laughed. "Touché."

He left her but not until kissing her until she almost asked him to stay. She did let him go, of course. She was willing to play with them, but not completely lose herself. She could do this—for a little while. To have two gorgeous men in the Caribbean? As Steffan had said, *sold.* She couldn't remember the last time she had one in her life beyond a night. Now, she had two.

## 26

Air conditioning was a crime in the tropics. Why bother being in St. Thomas if she was going to sit in recycled, reconditioned air? Hot weather meant she could be deliciously nude—as she had been all afternoon. They'd arrived at Regal Resorts in one of Alexander's private jets—Alexander, she, Steffan and Laurent, along with Jonathan and Christiana. The young woman finally relaxed with every mile put between them and Washington, D.C. Sarah, herself, had blissfully curled into one of the over-sized recliners on the plane while Laurent kneaded her feet. Steffan had sprawled on the opposite side and regaled her of tales of summers in his family's cottage on Gotland where apparently half of Sweden goes when "worshipping summer" as he put it. She understood the delight in his eyes at talking about warmer weather when one is so tired of boots, coats, scarves—and in the Swede's case—a lack of sunlight.

Now the sun hung low over the Caribbean water, red, orange and yellow bands growing more pronounced in the fading blue sky. She curled her fingers around the brass railing of their balcony and forced herself to acknowledge all this was real.

A warm male body pressed against her back. "Spectacular view." Steffan's arm went around her, his other hand holding up a flute of orange juice.

"It is." She accepted the offered glass.

"The ocean and sky are nice, too." He nipped her shoulder.

She took a sip of the drink. "A mimosa?"

"I know how you like champagne, and getting enough Vitamin C is important."

"Where is Laurent?"

"Still asleep. I do believe we wore him out."

"Well, there was no time like the present to get started." A loud slap and moan echoed underneath their balcony. "Everyone else is."

Last night they'd had another evening of sex at her home, and then as soon as they'd arrived, she'd tied Laurent's wrists to the bedposts and proceeded to have sex with Steffan on the dresser facing the end of the bed. The large mirror over the bureau allowed him to see everything—front and back, and while she hadn't believed she possessed an exhibitionist streak, she did like seeing Laurent's eyes fire as she watched him over Steffan's shoulder. Afterward, she let Laurent have a taste of her while fisting his own cock to completion—on his knees in the shower.

"So this weekend will be nothing but debauchery and pleasure?" he asked. "Sounds like Laurent and I are going to enjoy our Accendos membership. It seems the entire club has moved here."

"It has, but now we have to get to Alexander's cocktail hour. We missed his opening lunch—"

"I missed lunch?" Laurent yawned and stepped out onto the balcony, fully nude.

"Don't worry, there's an open buffet 24/7 by the pool. No one will go hungry this weekend."

He grinned at her and squinted out over the water. "Wow. I say we never go back to Sweden."

"And give up those days of no sunlight and eight feet of snow?"

"Sadist," Laurent said.

A loud knock sounded at the door.

"You won't go hungry today," Steffan strode through the balcony door. "I ordered you one of everything on the menu while you were out."

"The man secretly loves me, what can I say?" Laurent shrugged.

Of course he did, and not so secretly. Steffan was physically comfortable with another male in a way that so many American men were not. He and Laurent exchanged touches with no hesitation, though she hadn't seen them have sex. She wouldn't mind watching them if they chose to. In the meantime, she was going to have to keep a close eye on Laurent who'd enchanted the front desk, the bellman, and everyone else he encountered from the time he got on the plane until he'd walked in the door to their room.

She stepped inside to find Steffan laughing at something said by the dark-skinned woman who pushed the tray closer to the center of the room. "Beautiful Madras."

The woman's smile revealed white teeth against her dark skin, clearly delighted by his reference to her dress. He had a way with people—like Laurent, but different. Steffan noticed everything about them, seemed generally interested in them.

Her admiration for these two men had moved into an entirely different realm. She felt her heart edging closer to a tipping point.

"May I take you to breakfast, Mistress?" Laurent

presented his elbow, as both of these men did so often for her.

"Breakfast?"

"It's Steffan's favorite meal of the day. He'll eat it anytime."

Those two really did know each other well.

She took his arm. "Laurent, after we eat, what do you say the three of us head down to the beach? Alexander won't mind if we miss this cocktail thing. The sunset will be beautiful to watch."

"I'd love it. Steffan is 'okay' in the water."

He laughed. "Okay, my ass."

The man hadn't been kidding. He'd ordered one of everything, so she did something she hadn't in years. She had a little bit of everything from all the plates—pancakes in warmed syrup and fresh blueberries, an egg-white omelet with Gruyere cheese, mushrooms, and chives, and Laurent fed her strawberries as she sipped a third Mimosa.

Even as her belly finally groaned in protest, she still found room for a few bites of a beignet, where she ended up wearing half the powdered sugar. Steffan kissed off the white dust on her lips and chin and poured her yet another Mimosa. She finally had to cry uncle.

"I'm afraid I won't fit into my bathing suit," she said.

"You brought a suit?" Steffan's horror made her laugh. His surprise wasn't unwarranted. Derek had closed the resort to anyone other than his and Alexander's guests, and Regal Resort's beaches were closed to the public.

"Well, that's disappointing," Steffan said. "I haven't swum with a suit in years."

"I haven't swum in years."

Both men looked at her aghast. "Get ready to end that record."

Laurent stood. "Mistress Sarah, will you do us the

extreme honor of accompanying us to the beach and oversee my first swim in the Caribbean Sea?" He extended his arm once more. She really could get used to this escort service.

She rose. "Only if you bring the champagne with you."

"Done and done." He pulled the bottle out of the ice bucket. "To hell with the shrinkage in front of my Mistress," Laurent called and raised the bottle.

She burst out laughing. "We'll reverse it later."

## 27

Laurent whooped and threw his entire body into the small wave.

"You have to forgive him," Steffan said, propped up on one elbow. "He's reliving his childhood summers in Barcelona. The water's a little cold in the North Atlantic for his taste."

"Come on, you two. Get in here," Laurent called.

Steffan waved to him.

"There isn't a negative bone in that man," she said absent-mindedly. She leaned back against the cushion of the chaise, feeling the sun beat down on her nude body. She'd let her gossamer sarong with the bright green and yellow hibiscus flowers fall open, and the ends now teased the sides of her legs in the slight breeze.

"He's the best man I've ever known," Steffan said.

"You're easy with him. But not lovers," she said. "You're unusual, Steffan Vidar."

"I'm Swedish. Americans are too uptight about gender roles."

"I have to agree, but some of us do find our way," she said.

"Alexander mentioned you two met in a club long ago."

"Yes. A horrible little public play space in southwest DC. I'm surprised it stayed open as long as it did. Thank god Alexander opened Accendos."

"He also said you thought you hurt someone once."

*He did what?* Every brain cell shouted in her head. Please, dear God, let this be a slip-up because she was not ready to go there, not when she felt so good.

"I'm just curious about you, Sarah, please don't take offense. I can't imagine you hurting anyone. You're too careful."

"Why do I feel that's not a compliment."

"It's not meant to be a criticism." He leaned back himself. "And I want you to know, I trust you. With me. With Laurent. In case there was any doubt."

"Thank you," she said.

"I hope you know you can trust us."

"It's a little late for this talk, don't you think?" she laughed, but it meant a lot to her that Steffan had said those words. It might be dangerous, to allow someone to dictate how she felt about herself, but for the moment, the sun was so warm, and with Laurent's whoops and calls for them to join them … Unhappiness wouldn't get a toehold in her this weekend.

Steffan stood and held out his hand. "He's not going to stop, you know. Laurent is as stubborn as we are in getting what we want."

She rose. She didn't need to say "no" to something fun to prove she was in control. That had never been her kind of dominance as so many new to the scene did—be contrarian and hard in order to prove they couldn't be bowled over.

She held his hand all the way into the water. The cold hit her skin, and a hit of aliveness woke her up to the center of her soul. Or perhaps it was the glee on Laurent's face as

Steffan dropped her hand and lurched toward him. The two men sprawled into the waves in an easy, male bonding thing that she'd never understood. Why the need to bash each other to show love? She didn't need to understand anything right now. Right now, she was happy.

Twenty minutes in the water and she began to fathom the joy she'd seen on children's faces as they surfed the water.

"Now remember," Steffan said, "Lie there like a sack of potatoes and let the wave do all the work. You just ride it. You don't need to swim it. Here comes another. Ready?"

"Okay." She put her back to the wave to try for the fifteenth time to ride one. She pushed off as Steffan had instructed—right at the point the wave was cresting one foot behind her. Delicious seawater ran through the center of her legs, over her breasts. This time, it floated her forward as if an invisible hand of Neptune himself cradled her in his open palm and delivered her to the beach.

As soon as the motion stopped going forward, she stumbled to her feet and turned. "I did it!" She pushed her way back toward them.

Laurent hoisted her up. "One for Mistress Sarah. Zero for the takedown!" He tossed her into the air and then she was underwater. She came up sputtering—to a horrified Laurent.

"Oh, Mistress I'm sorry."

She coughed and splashed him. "I'm so going to punish you for that."

"Promise?" The eagerness in his voice was palpable.

She pushed herself through the water to him and cupped his cheek. "I promise, lovely Laurent." She kissed him fully and hard. He seemed taken aback at first but then kissed her back thoroughly. He was another good kisser. A wave threatened to destroy their balance, but Steffan's arms were right there, steadying them. When she released his lips, Laurent's eyes were ringed with emotion.

"I—"

She placed a finger over his lips. "I know." They stayed like that, arms around one another, for a few minutes. It was oddly comfortable, being pulled further into the sea and then bobbing up and down in the waves. Steffan tightened his grip on the two of them.

"Did you know that every seventh wave is larger than the other six?" Laurent asked. "Count them. This one was number five," he said as he bobbed upward, taking her with him.

When another wave took them up, Steffan whispered *six* in her ear. When the seventh wave took them even higher, all three of them rising in the cold, salty water, she felt a prickle behind her eyelids. She had a curious sensation that she was feeling the earth all around her and its natural rhythm—like ocean waves that followed a pattern. She breathed in, and for the first time in too many months, she felt connected to something—and two someones.

A loud splash and cry from a woman had them turning their heads. Another couple had jumped into the waves together. Spell broken, she suddenly had to pee.

"Well, gentleman, I must run to the ladies' room," she said.

"You're in the ocean," Steffan said.

"No way. I'll be right back."

They may have gotten her into the ocean, but she drew the line at peeing there.

She pushed her way through waves that tried hard to get her to stay and jogged up to grab her sarong—for whatever reason she'd never know. Half the resort walked around nude. The thin fabric clung to her wet body as she forced her sandy feet into her flip-flops and made her way to the ladies' room by the pool. She was wrong. By the play happening in and around the pool, more like three-fourths of the resort were now fully nude. A volleyball game was in full swing, and in one of the white canvas cabanas, a man had a woman draped over his arm and was delivering a hard spanking.

She found herself alone in the ladies' room. One look in the mirror and she didn't recognize herself. Mascara ringed under her eyes, her hair in its inadequate ponytail looked like a drowned rat's tail. She moved to pull the elastic out and found it wasn't going to budge easily. Shit, she should go up to her room and put herself back together.

After doing her business—because there was no way she'd make it to her room without doing so—she rounded the corner and ran smack into a wall of Alexander.

"Sarah?" He held her arms, keeping a foot distance between them. She couldn't blame him. He wore a stunning white linen shirt and khaki pants—the billionaire's beach look. She'd have gotten him soaked.

"Hi, Alexander."

His face stretched into a huge grin. "Having fun?"

"Steffan and Laurent insisted I go into the ocean." She laughed lightly. "Can you believe it? Me?"

"That's wonderful. I haven't been in the ocean in years. You may have inspired me."

"Well if you do, I recommend Steffan's body surfing lessons."

Alexanders' hearty laugh warmed her a little. "I may have to do that. I'm so glad they're here with you, Sarah." He leaned down—he was so tall—and said. "I heartily approve."

"Don't read too much into it, Alexander. We finally worked out an arrangement that could work."

"It's enough for you?"

"Believe I need more men?"

"If anyone could handle more, you could. Well, I can't keep my guests waiting any longer."

"I'm sorry we're not there, Alexander."

"Don't be silly. It's more important to be where you are. I'll see you later." He winked.

Guilt rose up in her. She'd been Alexander's right-hand person—in a way—for so long; she should be supporting him —not indulging in body surfing and tanning. Here she was acting like an ordinary guest when she wasn't ordinary. Nothing about her life was. It wasn't a pretentious thought, but rather the truth. She wasn't better. She was just more careful.

She headed back to the beach. It was time for them to rejoin the party—the whole party.

## 28

Sarah stepped up to the mirror as she fastened the long, thin gossamer strand of gold into her ear that teased the tops of her shoulders. Laurent waited for her acknowledgment. Her lashes raised and a relaxed smile played on her lips in the mirror when she saw him.

"Thank you, Laurent."

He'd brought her the shoes she'd requested—sandals with a lower heel than he'd ever seen her wear, but still a two-inch heel.

"No death heels tonight," Steffan leaned against the door frame, a formal jacket over his t-shirt.

She smiled over at him, something she was doing more of now on a regular basis. "They don't go with this dress," she said. "But I did bring some for later." She winked at Laurent and his pride swelled.

She'd kissed him today full on the mouth. He'd been stunned by that move, felt his heart move under his chest in a way he didn't think possible. He was in love with her. Steffan was as well. They could do this, all three of them. Laurent had loved seeing her let go in the ocean today. Hair plastered against her head, her mouth in an "O" as the wave carried her to shore. He wondered what she was like as a young girl—that much vitality now unleashed in girlhood?

Steffan pushed off. "This came," Steffan said in the doorway, holding out a small cream-colored envelope. Her first initial only - S - was written in an elegant hand across the front.

"An invitation already?"

"Invitation?" Laurent asked.

"Alexander loves the formality of things. I recognize his handwriting." She walked into the large living area, slitting open the envelope with her nail.

*It's time. For both of us.*

"Mysterious." Steffan read over her shoulder.

"Yes, Alexander loves his mystery." Her brow furrowed as she placed the note on the coffee table. "Well, ready?"

Laurent glanced at the message. He could only hope what he read meant Alexander was going to finally do what he'd hoped. They were so close, so very close.

# 29

Sarah nodded at the gentleman dressed in black, wearing a black mask, who held open the door for her. They immediately paused inside the main doorway to Alexander's official birthday celebration.

"Wow," Laurent said.

"Alexander certainly knows how to throw a party," Steffan said.

Sarah smiled at her two dumbstruck males. "He enjoys ceremony and opulence."

"Master, Mistress." A statuesque blond woman wearing a slick, red bodysuit that upon closer inspection was nothing but body paint, held out a tray of champagne flutes, tumblers, and goblets holding various drinks.

"Something for everyone?" Steffan asked as he plucked a champagne flute off the tray for Sarah and a Scotch—at least he thought it was Scotch—for himself. Laurent waved off the offer of something to drink. From the size of the man's eyes, the sight before him would capture him wholly in for a while.

The room was actually three ballrooms opened to one

another to create one large space. Specially designed furniture, St. Andrews' crosses, water tanks, and suspension units filled the area, with the hundreds of guests dispersed throughout, some in full play, others in conversation. Two redheaded men, who looked like twins, flogged a man to their left. A man in a tuxedo caressed a woman in suspension to their left.

"Disneyland for the kinky," Steffan declared.

Sarah laughed. "Care to walk around?"

"Love to." He took her hand and pulled her close. Laurent fell in step behind them as they traversed the expansive space.

"Derek could hold an event for three thousand people here," Steffan said.

"Yes, and it's perfect for three hundred who require a wide berth."

"Alexander does give quite a nod to the Greek Gods," he said absentmindedly. Several large fountains with statues of Greek Gods—one placed in every third of the space—lorded over the crowd.

They paused at the first fountain, where a woman was pilloried between two statues of young Greek men facing one another. Each of the statues wore collars with rings dangling from the center like pendants, and the woman's arms were stretched out, each cuffed wrist hooked to those rings. Her cuffed ankles received similar treatment, spread wide and connected to eyebolts in the base. Her diaphanous dress was soaked and clung to her so Steffan could make out the hard points of her nipples and the delicate folds of her pussy quivering as a man stood behind her, whispering and caressing the shell of her ear. The lightest touches were often felt the most, and when Steffan pulled Sarah a little closer to him, she let him. She trembled slightly, a mix of the sight and Steffan's hand lazily drawing circles on the curve of her hip.

She peered up at him. "Laurent would look amazing in that position."

"He would." He glanced back at his friend close behind them. Steffan nodded once, and Laurent's body met her back. She murmured at the contact, enjoying his warmth, his smell. She brought Steffan's hand up to her lips and sucked on the tip of his forefinger.

"Let see what else Alexander has in store for us," she said.

They walked for many more minutes, stopping occasionally to say hello to a friend but mostly moved slowly from scene to scene, letting the energy seep into them. At each stop, Laurent and Steffan drew her between them, and she relished that maleness engulfing her. The room had grown exceptionally warm, despite the constant air conditioning tumbling over them in a frosty white mist overhead. Sweat, male musk, colognes, and perfumes mixed and mingled and the slaps and delighted moans filled the space until the room was a symphony of pleasure.

Music thrummed from unseen speakers, a mix of electronic chill with enough beat to keep up the energy but enough melody to be pleasing. The thumps of the music coursed through the soles of her feet and up her legs, and she grew impatient watching all this play with Steffan's warm hand engulfing hers, Laurent trailing behind them.

They stopped at the largest fountain in the middle where a woman lay face down on a spider web of chain links suspended over the largest foundation. Curls of water hit her in various places—her breasts, her legs, and occasionally her pussy.

"Like what you see? I know how you like water," Steffan chuckled.

"It's ingenious," she said. Before she could step closer, a familiar voice called her name.

"Sarah." Jonathan stood a few feet away. They strode to

where he conversed with a couple she didn't recognize. Christiana was so tightly banded to his side she was surprised not to find a diamond-encrusted leash around his fiancé.

She kissed her stepbrother on the cheeks and gave Christiana a hug. "You look beautiful as always," she told the young girl, who did who did indeed stunned in a midnight blue bandage wrap dress. So much for her not wanting something tight.

"Thank you. Jonathan picked it out." She looked up at him and smirked good-naturedly.

"Where's the guest of honor? I haven't seen Alexander," Sarah asked.

"Turn around." Jonathan inclined his head to a point behind her.

It was then Sarah tuned into the tittering all around her. She pivoted in time to see Alexander stripping off his shirt, tossing it to a woman, and walking—shirtless—to the large podium which featured the water torture feature. He couldn't be. Sarah hadn't seen him play in years. Yes, that's right, she thought. It had been years. Why hadn't she thought to question him why before now?

A man, marked as one of tonight's slaves by his head-to-toe black clothing and mask, jogged up to the steps, dropped to one knee, and presented a worn, black flogger on the palms of his hands. Alexander peered down at the man, grasped the handle and let the long tails trail over the man's open palms. The slave shuddered—whether at the sensation or the fact Alexander had caused it, she couldn't say.

"Thank you, slave," Alexander said.

The man's lips parted in pleasure at his acknowledgment.

Alexander didn't seem to realize he'd attracted a crowd. Instead, he homed in on the woman at the center of the spider web. He circled her until he got to her head. The water jets stopped, the burble of water replaced by the music instead. He crouched and whispered. The woman shuddered, but Sarah caught a slight nod. Whatever Alexander had asked of the woman, she'd given her consent. Alexander held out his hand, and the woman strained to reach out and kiss his knuckles.

Sarah's foot kicked the base of the bottom step, and she quickly scanned the crowd. She'd unconsciously moved forward until she was the base of the podium, now ringed with observers. Their own play had likely halted the second Alexander stepped up the two stairs to the pedestal holding the large fountain.

Alexander rose and walked to a starting position. He tested the weight of the handle of the flogger, and Sarah almost couldn't believe her eyes. *He was going to do it.* He pulled the flogger back and cast the long tails forward. The tips landed sharply on a woman's back, and she shuddered. The chain links of the spider web on which she lay clanked under her movement.

Alexander had named the flogger, the Contessa, years ago as a long-standing joke between him and a past lover. Sarah was one of the few privileged to ever hear the story. It was long and sad, and she couldn't think about it now, not when the man who was the single greatest influence in her life stood there, magnificent, confident and with such certainty, she understood the message to everyone in the room. Whatever had kept him from publicly playing was now over.

*Over.* His note's message floated across her mind. *It's time.* Was this what he'd meant? She forced herself to look away for one second to scan the crowd that had drifted toward the scene in a cloud of diamonds, gowns, and nudity. Like a magnet, Alexander had transfixed all three hundred people who had left D.C. for St. Thomas to honor the man who turned sixty today.

"You didn't know either, did you?" Jonathan had sidled up next to her. She turned to see his eyes, an understanding passing between them that he hadn't been expecting this, either. He, of all people, would grasp the pivotal moment they witnessed. Alexander was playing publicly for the first time in over a decade. *Ten years.*

"I've never seen him out of a business suit," Christiana's voice floated to her ears.

Sarah was vaguely aware of London and Carson standing nearby. Sarah couldn't rip her gaze from Alexander, now flogging the woman hard and fast while groans emanated from her lips.

"I've never seen him from behind a desk—how can he ... oh, my God ... He must work out with Marcos," Christiana said.

"There's no way that chest belongs to a sixty-year-old," London added.

"Sixty is the new fifty or in his case, the new forty," Christiana said. "I mean, look at him."

The rest of their conversation was lost to her as she tuned into the deep thud of the flogger snapping backward and forward, again and again, landing perfect hits that left long red stripes on the beautiful woman's back. The woman who gripped the metal links sighed contentedly. The links had to bite into her skin.

Despite the mask he wore, a tall man Sarah recognized as Eric Morrison, stood a few feet away, mesmerized by Alexander. Sarah knew Eric had been after Alexander for years, though Alexander had shown nothing but polite acknowledgment to anyone in all the time she'd known him. And, she and Alexander had known each other for decades. He'd known her when she wasn't as she was now—ordered, disciplined, responsible.

She'd played hard during her first decade in the lifestyle.

There was a time she couldn't get enough, learn enough, try out enough things. Then, the unthinkable happened. She'd hurt someone. Thank god Alexander stepped in when he had. He had mentored her through that lost and angry time. As she discovered bits and pieces of herself, she built a set of rules like someone builds a house—one board at a time. She learned to *channel* herself.

She'd helped him, too. She worked hard to assist him as he built Club Accendos and the Tribunal and believed in its order, its purpose, and its gift to the people in the lifestyle.

She grew dizzy with the realization of how quickly time had passed. Steffan's hand landed on her hip as if to steady her, and when she leaned backward, she met the hard muscle of Laurent's chest. They'd closed in to support her.

Alexander laid his hand on the woman's wet, dark curls, his palm so large it covered her head. He murmured something to her, and Sarah was sure the woman purred a response. Sarah's eyes grew wet with the beauty of the scene and threatened to flow when Alexander himself, untied the knots that bound her to the contraption. The web was righted with the help of two assistants. Alexander gently placed her into the arms of two submissive assistants. Propped up between them now, he took both of her hands into one of his, tipped her chin up with the other. "Thank you," he said. The woman's eyes were glazed, but Sarah knew she'd remember those words, the pride in his eyes at her service.

He then turned, chest rising and falling still from exertion, and looked down at her. She'd gotten close, probably too close, and her shoulders tightened ever so slightly.

"Sarah," he whispered and held out his hand. A kick of complicated emotions—awe, thrill, fear, love—intruded on her composure, and she had to clear her throat. She stepped up the three wide steps and took his hand.

She had zero romantic interest in Alexander, and he felt similarly toward her, but she drank in the sight of him—his silver hair, deep blue eyes, and a six-foot-five frame that towered over most people. They had been so much more to each other than mere lovers. She had never felt small in his presence, never felt less than him. That was his rare gift, she supposed, making others feel worthy no matter the truth.

He turned her palm so it faced up and ran his thumb along her wrist line—something he'd never done. "You got my note."

She swallowed. "Yes."

"Good. You know my past, and I know yours. It's time to put it where it belongs—behind us. Now, you're going to do something for me."

"Anything, Alexander." Why was she so damned emotional?

"Stop holding yourself back. Fall in love." When his lips quirked upward into a rare, full smile, she felt the full weight of his words.

Her eyes stung with pending tears. "I do love … Laurent." She could admit that. Who couldn't love that man who now knelt at the base of the podium? His ability to give was unfathomable.

"That's a good first step. Be willing to keep going." He leaned down to whisper in her ear. "You've never harmed anyone in your life … not even back then, and you won't now. Trust him. Trust both of them."

A tidal wave of memory threatened to drown her. She knew what he was saying—let go of what Joshua did. Let go of what had happened when he found her in that dungeon. But how could she?

"What if I can't?" she said.

"Then trust them to show you how." He released her hand

and then beckoned for Steffan to join them. "The note wasn't just for you."

*S.* It never occurred to her the note could have been for Sarah or Steffan—or as Alexander had just said, for both of them.

Alexander looked over her shoulder. She turned to find Laurent, kneeling at the base of the steps. "Laurent," Alexander's voice boomed. "Your Master and Mistress have need of you." He turned back to Sarah. "Trust. We're nothing without it."

Steffan's ice blue eyes found her, along with his hand, which he placed on the small of her back—not declaring ownership but rather something more important. He wanted to support her. He had never tried to turn her into something she wasn't, someone who *needed* his reassurance. Yet, there he was, giving it to her anyway.

"Laurent," Steffan said. "Now." Laurent swiftly rose and climbed the stairs. He'd not moved until he heard Steffan's voice.

"No," she said when he moved to kneel before Alexander. "Before me." Alexander was right. It was time to move forward—with these two men. She'd made a mistake long ago, and she'd been punishing herself ever since. Why?

"Alexander," Steffan said. "Happy Birthday."

The man chuckled. "It will be very happy if you promise me something."

"Never harm Sarah."

"Or Laurent." The man's eyes flicked downward to where the beautiful submissive knelt.

"Alexander, if Sarah or Laurent were ever to come to harm because of me, well ..." He looked at her. "I wouldn't be able to live with myself."

Her stomach lurched. Memories could cut as sure as a knife, and she felt the slice of his words as if he'd taken a machete to her heart. That agony she'd leashed over the years, the remorse she'd boxed up so carefully, burst out so violently she struggled to stay upright. She absolutely believed him. A few minutes ago she was facing one direction, and with those words—*I wouldn't be able to live with myself*—the past spun her around. She'd let her guard down, and she'd been punished for it. Steffan wouldn't know what his words meant, but they hit her dead center. *Shattering.* She honest-to-god felt her heart splinter into pieces.

Steffan's hands were reaching for her, but she couldn't let him touch her. "Steffan, I ... need a minute."

It was such a lie. No amount of time was going to fix this.

# 30

Sarah spun and jogged down the steps, pushing past people who'd gathered to watch Alexander. She even bumped into one of the dungeon monitors, a man in a black tee-shirt that strained around biceps and chest muscles, his eyes visible through a black mask.

Steffan turned to a stone-faced Alexander. "What was that?"

"Go after her." Alexander wrapped a hand around his bicep. "Ask her about Joshua Martin and Troy Myers."

Steffan jumped down the steps, nearly knocking a man into two women. The crowd was thick. Men and women in various states of dress—or wholly nude—had resumed their conversations, their playing, their flirting, oblivious to what occurred. Hell, he didn't know what had happened. What had he said? *I wouldn't be able to live with myself.* An exclamation to grind the seriousness of how much he felt about her, but somehow that statement induced a crushing agony in her eyes, trembling in her lips.

He was vaguely aware of Laurent behind him, and God love the man, Laurent kept in stride with him as he sprinted between people. He had no idea where Sarah would head. Then by the grace of God, he saw her dart through the ballroom doors about forty feet away. Before they snapped shut again, he caught a glimpse of her heading straight for a set of glass doors that led to a terrace and the beach.

He caught Laurent's ashen face as he pushed through the doors.

"What happened?" Laurent asked.

He wished he knew.

It wasn't hard to find her. She sat on the sand, halfway down to the water, staring out calmly, as if she hadn't just bolted from Alexander Rockingham himself, through a crowd of three hundred guests with the two of them giving them chase. Tiki torches lining the walkways, a few dotting the sand, illuminated her form. Her knees were pulled up under her chin, her long diaphanous gown whipping in the wind, tendrils of brown hair rising and swirling in the air currents. She looked like a goddess summoning a storm. He kicked off his shoes and strode toward her. His heavy breathing from the chase could be heard over the rumble of the ocean waves.

He stood over her, while Laurent fell to his knees. The sand was cold under his feet, in contrast to the heat of the air.

"Sarah—"

"When did you know you were a Dominant?" she asked, not looking up at them.

"What's wrong, Tell me."

She turned her face up to him, a sheen of unshed tears glistening in her eyes, the firelight from tiki torches sharpening the angles in her face.

"When?" she asked again.

"College. I think. It was slow." He dropped to his butt next to her. "Why is this important?"

She took a deep breath. "I always ask in interviews, and your answer is telling. If you answer 'always,' it tells me two things: you started at least thinking about dominance at a young age and two, you might be reckless. If you say 'I've always been a little bossy, but I didn't start feeling sexually Dominant until later, and then when I found the scene, I felt at home,' that tells me you might have taken your time."

Why was she explaining this to him?

"Okay then. I guess I can't pinpoint exactly when," he said. "Now what happened back there."

"I was fourteen when I realized I was a sexual Dominant. I always knew I was powerful. My father was the first person to tell me I had to be careful. He said, 'Sarah, you are able to make people do things. Be careful what you ask for.' I was seven. Funny how you never forget some things, but I can't remember what his hands looked like." She turned to Laurent. "Isn't that odd?"

He swallowed. "No. I can't remember what my mother's voice sounded like. It's disconcerting."

She placed her hand on his arm and gave him a sad smile. "Yes. Then there are some things you try hard to forget and you can't."

"Who are Joshua Martin and Troy Myers?" Steffan asked.

Her gaze darted to his face. "Who told you those names?" Her voice, stronger and tinged with anger, told him she wasn't completely gone.

"Alexander."

She swallowed. "He wouldn't."

"He just did." Steffan settled closer to her. "These men hurt you."

Her mouth twisted into a slow, sad smile ."No. It was very much the other way around." Sarah dug her toes in the sand. "I knew there was no getting out of this weekend without remembering. Tomorrow is the anniversary of … Joshua. But it was the price I was willing to pay for my loyalty to Alexander, to show up here and honor the man who's been the single most important influence in my life. And"—She looked at Laurent—"The two of you were going to be with me."

"We are with you." Laurent took her hand. "Sarah. Mistress, please."

She intertwined her hand into his, then reached for Steffan's and did the same. "I'm going to tell you something." Her throat clenched, the muscles taut against her words. "And when I do, know there is always a jet waiting to take you back."

"Fat chance of that happening."

She gave him a wavering smile but then returned her attention to the water. "We'll see. Joshua Martin was the son of the most elegant woman I'd ever known. Clementina Delvecchio Martin. She was so nurturing, so much more of a mother than Claire Marillioux ever was. Clementina gave me my first Hermes scarf. She taught me about clothes and cultivated a sense of style in me—all done with the greatest love. In many ways, she made me the stylist I am today. I adored her—loved her far more than I loved my own mother. She and her husband, James, were friends of my mother's and Jonathan's father … maybe. Or had they met when my mother was married to Harold?" She shook her head. "Who can remember which husband." She rested her chin on her knees.

"They had one child, a son, Joshua. A golden boy. Tall. Handsome. Smart. Athletic. So very, very gentle and kind. There wasn't anything he didn't excel at, and he adored me. All through high school, we were a 'thing.' He was my first—everything. First date. First dance. First kiss. First lover … first submissive. He was more than willing to help me explore that side of my sexuality. He got off on it, too."

She paused and swallowed, angrily swiped at a tear that had run down her cheek. She then straightened and drew in a long breath.

"Josh had a full scholastic scholarship to Harvard. Pre-law, though he would have made an awful lawyer," she laughed. "Not nearly cut-throat enough. I told him he should go for pre-med. Pediatrics. He would have been great with kids. Josh begged me to go to Harvard with him. He wanted us to go to school together, get married, settle in DC and have a family. Stay close to his parents. Clementina and James would have been over the moon, but they never pushed. It would have been the perfect fairytale ending ... for everyone but me." She pulled her other hand free and placed both in her lap.

"I was seventeen and even then realized I didn't love Joshua in the way he loved me. I didn't want any of the things he wanted. I wanted to go to New York. I wanted to work in design. Wanted to travel. Explore the club scene ... explore *other* men." She took a deep, steadying breath. "I think I was the first and only thing in his life he really wanted he couldn't have. He was devastated, but I thought ... he'd get over me. Find some nice girl at Harvard. It's what people do, right? They move on."

She shuddered, and he barely restrained himself from gathering her into his arms.

"So, I left for Vassar. He went to Cambridge. I did miss him, just not in the way he missed me. I was so excited to be so close to New York City." Her eyes glazed as she stared into nothing. "Almost every weekend I took the train into the city and explored the club scene. It was like ... a whole new world for me. Then I came home for Thanksgiving. Joshua invited me over to have dinner with his family. I was happy to accept. When I got to their house ..."

A strangled cry erupted in her throat, and by the way her

neck strained, the way her hands balled into fists, she was fighting to not break down. "It was so dark. No lights in the windows, nothing to show that anyone was home. I let myself in. I'd always had a key. I figured there had been some miscommunication. Maybe I had gotten the time wrong. I walked through the house, calling, and … I found him." She halted and took a huge steadying breath. "I found him hanging from the light fixture in his room. I called 911 but …" She shook her head and tears streamed freely down her cheeks. "Clementina and James arrived with the paramedics. He'd left a note."

Her voice dropped to a flat whisper as if reciting from memory. *"You never believed me when I said I couldn't live in this world without you. Always remember I loved you more than life itself."*

"It was the worst day of my life. Either before or since, except when … they found the pictures in his duffle bag. Joshua liked me to take polaroids of him when he was bound. Clementina and James never needed to know that. They should never have had those images be the last memory of Joshua. If nothing else it was a hideous reminder of the final rope around his neck. The scandal was horrific. I can still see the headlines in bold font, Prominent Family's Son Suicides Over Teenage Lover. James burned the pictures in the bathroom sink and Clementina accused me of killing her son. They never spoke to me again. They sold the house and moved from Washington DC. I was shipped back to Vassar in disgrace, told to stay away for a few years. I deserved far worse than banishment."

"Sarah." He didn't hide the empathy in his voice. "It wasn't your fault; you know that. You were so young."

She shook her head and stared at the ocean. "I should have seen it coming. I should have done more … I was closer to Joshua than anyone in the world. I was responsible for him. I should have done more." She ground out those last words as if trying to etch them into her soul.

"Mistress," Laurent began.

"Please, Laurent. Don't." She held up her hands, then dropped them into her lap again.

Steffan took a deep breath. "I wouldn't ask you if Alexander hadn't insisted ... but ..."

She sighed. "Troy Myers."

"Yes." He took her hand, uncurled her tense fingers and held them in his larger palm. "You can tell me. Us." Despite the misery etched across Laurent's face at this new information, he wanted him included.

"Troy was a sub I met in Washington, after I came back. I had to, you know, for Jonathan. I couldn't leave him to those vipers," she spat. "And I couldn't stop being who I was. So I went a little wild, dabbled in the DC scene, and met Troy in the same club where I met Alexander Rockingham. At that time, rules and protocol didn't carry the same weight they do today. Very little was controlled. No vetting for mental stability or personality disorders. Troy and I scened a few times, and he became obsessed with me. I tried to end it because I knew how dangerous obsession could become. Instead of making it better, he got worse. One night, he brought a gun to the club and threatened me with it and then turned it on himself. He blew his brains all over the wall, not two feet from where I stood. Alexander was there. I'd barely known the man, and he just ... steps in. Who does that?"

"Alexander," Laurent whispered.

"Yes." She glanced at him briefly. "He got me legal counsel to clear my involvement, kept me out of the papers. That last part won my mother's favor. I'll tell you that. Alexander worked on the Hill then, and he cashed in every chit he had for me, said he knew what it was like to have the world turn its back on you." She cleared her throat. "I don't know what I would have done without Alexander. I was so messed up after that. I don't know that I would ever have gotten straightened out if it weren't for him."

She turned to face him. "So now you know. You ask why so many rules? I turned to discipline and strict order out of necessity. I need protocol and distance so that people don't get hurt. I won't let anyone grow too close again because Clementina had it right. I'm a killer."

He circled his arm around her. "No, Sarah, you weren't a killer. You never could be."

"Never," Laurent took her hand and kissed her knuckles.

She huffed, delicately, and shook her head. It was her eyes that concerned him, however. They'd grown flat once more as if mesmerized by something in the distance. Melancholy and regret, he thought bitterly. Those were the real killers of life. They snuck up on you, hung around until they were wormed their way inside and breached your molecules. Sarah stared out at the water, and by the anguish in her face, she didn't have regrets. They had her.

Laurent shifted in the sand and drew closer.

"That was the seventh," she said suddenly. She'd been counting the waves.

"One," Laurent said as the next roll of ocean water crested and fell to the beach.

She looked over at him and smiled. Steffan caught the glint of moonlight in a sheen of tears when she turned her gaze back to the water.

"Two," she said.

For over an hour, they watched the ocean waves, numbers the only words spoken. The moon's reflection danced along the ripples in the ocean, but nothing inside Steffan calmed. He'd meant what he'd said. He'd kill anything that harmed Sarah. But how do you kill ghosts?

## 31

For the first time in his life, Laurent was afraid to touch a woman. He wanted to hold Sarah—press her against him, kiss every inch of that worried face, erase all that stress thrumming through her body. He was afraid she might shatter upon contact. Steffan was braver than he. He'd had Sarah in the crook of his arm all the way from the beach, across terraces and marble floors, and up the elevator and down the hallway, never letting an inch separate their bodies.

As soon as they entered the suite, however, Sarah pushed herself free and pointed at the second bedroom.

"That bedroom is open for you both." She then disappeared into the room they'd been sharing and clicked the door shut, the lock sounding a second later.

Tension rose in the cords of Steffan's neck, his hands clenched by his sides. The man was used to action. He stormed down doors when they were shut in your face as he had in Amsterdam. Restraint cost him, especially when someone he loved suffered.

"Drink?" Laurent asked and strode to the bar across the room. He didn't know what else to do.

"You don't drink."

"I do now." He pulled the stopper off the bottle holding clear liquid, not really caring what it held and poured a fingerful into a tumbler. He handed it to Steffan who waved it off. "Not vodka. I'll take Scotch."

Laurent downed the vodka and winced at the burn in his throat. It'd been over a year since he'd touched alcohol and even then it had been more to rid himself of the stench of beer and bourbon that permeated that house in Amsterdam than for any other reason. He poured Steffan's Scotch and brought it to him. The man, who he'd never before seen defeated, sat on the couch, head in his hands. He took the offered glass but didn't drink.

Laurent sighed and sat next to him. "What's next?"

"Hell if I know."

"That's the first time I've ever heard you say that."

"This is my first time falling in love with a female Dominant. The woman is being unreasonable. She has no right to believe that was her fault."

"Harsh."

"Truth." He kicked back the Scotch and hissed between his teeth. "So young and everyone around her believed—"

"I'm not sure that's the case. I overheard Claire …"

White hot anger filled Steffan's eyes at the mention of Sarah's mother.

"I believe Claire loves her daughter," Laurent continued. "I overheard her say to Sarah whatever happened with Joshua wasn't her fault. I didn't know what any of it meant at the time, but I believed her intent."

"Generous of you."

"She's still an evil bitch for letting Sarah's guilt fester."

Steffan huffed. "You got that right."

"I doubt Claire even knows about Troy Myers." Laurent

sighed. "I don't see how Sarah can blame herself, but you know Mistress. Once she gets an idea into her head—"

"She doesn't let go." Steffan shook his head and downed the vodka.

"She said she knew she was a Dominant from age fourteen. I suppose she has always been convinced she should be able to control everyone and everything around her. Why *would* she believe those close to her when they said these deaths weren't her fault? She believes everything is her responsibility to fix. Look at how she operates. She doesn't shy away from a challenge, that's for sure."

Steffan nodded his head, his eyes glazed as if in deep thought.

"Then she needs a greater responsibility, an opportunity for redemption, an opportunity to balance the scale."

Steffan looked at him, a smile growing on his face. "You're fucking brilliant."

"You're just getting this?"

"Laurent." He stood. "Up for a little castle storming?"

"Going to break down another door?" As he had in Amsterdam—literally?

"I need to do something, but only if you're okay with it." Laurent's back straightened in response to Steffan's take-no-prisoners tone. Steffan eyed the balcony that wrapped around the corner of their suite. "I'm going to go see if her slider door is open. I want to tell her about Amsterdam—what really happened."

"What happened. You mean how I got there?" Emotion choked Laurent's throat.

He scrubbed his hair. "Never mind. It's too much to ask."

Laurent rose to his feet. "No, it's a good plan. It would come out eventually."

"I want you to be there." Steffan slapped him on the

shoulder. "It's your story to tell, but I think it would help her if I told her."

"It'll piss her off."

"Exactly."

He shrugged. "Not sure I get the plan, but I trust you."

Steffan stilled. "Thank you for that."

"You saved my life." It was true. Steffan had, factually and figuratively. He owed his friend this gift to bare his darkest moment to help heal another's dark moment.

"Let's go save another," Steffan said.

The humid air slapped Laurent in the face as soon as he stepped out on to the balcony, and damn if Steffan wasn't right. Her sliding glass door was open a sliver as if she wanted to listen to the ocean waves. Light seeped through the crack of the bathroom door. They stepped inside, Steffan leading the way. The roar of water from inside the bathroom competed with the roar of the ocean behind them.

Steffan knocked on the door frame.

"No, Laurent. I don't need anything." Her voice was weary.

Steffan pushed open the door and leaned against the frame. "Oh, I'd say you need something all right."

She lay in a full bath, chin deep in milky water, her head against a towel. Lavender and eucalyptus scents drifted around his head. She was trying to calm herself? He was about to provoke the opposite feelings in her.

"Steffan, didn't I say—"

"You did, but we need to tell you something, and then you can kick us out. It's about Amsterdam." They moved inside. Steffan crossed his arms and leaned against the sink. Laurent went with his gut and knelt by the side of the tub. The tile bit into his knees, but it kept his awareness sharp.

"Steffan, can't this wait until morning?" she sighed.

"No. You know Laurent's parents died in a car accident."

She gaped at him.

"What you don't know is Laurent was driving."

Fuck, that hurt. Laurent cleared his throat. Sarah's wet hand came down on his forearm.

"Laurent." The sympathy in her voice only ratcheted up the emotion clogging his throat. Jesus, he hoped Steffan knew what he was doing.

"Look at me," she said.

He did what she asked. He'd do *anything* she asked.

"I don't know what Steffan is trying to pull here, but an accident—"

"Is another tragedy that wasn't anyone's fault." Steffan's voice was even, measured. "But, you see, our man Laurent here didn't believe that. Like you didn't believe Joshua Martin and Troy Myers—and yes, Sarah I'm going to say their names—took their own lives *of their own accord.*"

Laurent sucked in a deep breath and kept his eyes trained on Sarah. "A drunk driver smashed into us. Not my fault, Sarah. I know that now."

"Of course it wasn't. It's not the same thing."

"No, it's not," Steffan answered. "But guilt takes no prisoners, has no discernment whatsoever. It lands in your body and sticks around until you kick it to the curb."

"That was harsh." She raised her chin.

"Yes, because I won't let guilt have you, Sarah like I wouldn't let it have Laurent. I found him in an Amsterdam basement, chained to a wall. He'd been there for twelve days, Sarah. He was half dead."

"Chained?" She squirmed and slid, fighting to stand up. Laurent got Steffan's plan. Anger was better than whatever memory she'd fallen into earlier in the evening. She'd shed her depression like a worn coat.

"Yes. Chained." Steffan ground out the words, his eyes glinting with his own emotion. Laurent gripped his knees as that foggy memory tried to rise up and drown him. It couldn't though. So much energy began bouncing between them, Laurent thought the wall tiles might crack.

"Some sadistic bastards put in him in a basement and chained him to a wall, and he let them do it *because he thought he deserved it*. Picture that."

Laurent couldn't breathe for a second.

"But I got him out. So if you think I'm afraid of some past ghosts, guess again. I wouldn't let Laurent disappear without a fight, and I sure as hell am not going to let you do it, either."

Her lip quivered, but she raised her chin. She stepped out of the tub, and Laurent jumped up to grab a towel for her. She angrily wrapped it around herself.

"I'm not one of your submissives," she bit out. "I don't cower, don't—"

"Thank god for that." Steffan stalked forward. "I don't know how or why any of this happened, Sarah, but I love you, and I won't let you suffer anymore."

She stepped backward. "Two Dominants—"

"Can never be a couple. Believe me, I've heard that from my own head. But I can—"

"Do what?"

"I can be with *you*. Laurent, too. Now the questions is, do you want us?"

"Do you?" Laurent asked.

They both looked down at him as if they'd forgotten he was there.

She took in a sudden breath, but she didn't say "no."

"That's all I needed to know." Steffan strode forward, cupped her face. "It's not possible for you to harm me, Sarah Marillioux, and I know you won't hurt Laurent. What I'm about to do is in both of our best interests." He kissed her, and she grasped his wrists but didn't push him back.

Laurent stood and went to them, shoving back the desire

to throw his arms around both of their bodies, to shield them from all the misery raised tonight. Steffan released her lips.

"Your arrogance never wanes," she whispered.

"Just the way you like it. We don't get to choose who we fall in love with. It just happens."

"Yes, we do choose."

"I don't happen to agree with you, but using your assertion, Joshua Martin had a choice just like Troy Myers had a choice."

Her jaw firmed with that bit of challenge. Laurent had always known Steffan was quick on the uptake, but, Jesus, it was like watching a brilliant attorney pick apart an opposing counsel's argument.

"If you believe you have a choice in who you love, then choose me," Steffan said. "Choose Laurent. Just … try it on." He dropped his hold on her face.

She looked at Laurent. "What do you want?"

Relief coursed through him. Steffan had won. They both had.

"I want both of you. I need both of you." She slipped by Steffan and strode to the doorway but paused. "You should have told me about Amsterdam, Steffan."

"Probably," he said.

"No promises." She threw off her towel, and they followed her into the bedroom—and the bed.

## 32

Of all the emotions Steffan had called up, she clung to the only one she was willing to acknowledge—a fierce desire for Laurent. *Chained to a basement wall?* Heads were going to roll. She'd make sure of it.

She settled on the edge of the bed and looked up at the two men who'd followed her. "Laurent, when you gave us your list of limits at Accendos, did you leave anything out?"

"Nothing. I swear. I've worked through a lot over the last year …" The words died in his throat as his gaze returned to her feet.

"Laurent, tell her," Steffan said.

"I don't remember much. They used drugs."

They'd drugged him. They had stripped him of his ability to consent—and to pull it back. *Fuck.* She was going to turn Amsterdam inside out until every single person who'd harmed this gorgeous creature was … what? Dead?

"They're in jail," Steffan said.

She glared at him, a fire burning through her logic until she was nothing but a mass of vengeful wrath.

"What? You think I'd kill them? I wanted to. Where they are is worse, and they'll stay there so long as I live."

"You should have told me." God, her teeth hurt from clenching them so hard.

Laurent nodded slowly. "Yes, we should have, but I've learned over the last year, Mistress, the past is in the past, and that's where it needs to stay. Remember I told you Steffan was a good Dom. He's been working with me, showing me accepting abuse isn't the same as serving. It's what we've been doing for the last year." His dark eyes filled with such attention and tenderness she wondered how anyone could harm this man. She drew in a long breath to release the madness his story had called up in her.

"Laurent." She presented her foot. "Mind?"

He dropped to his knees and cradled her heel.

"Your fingers are magic," she said. "This is the way you can serve me." It also would help calm the rising vengeance she felt. She had resources. She had access to *people* who could infiltrate governments, prisons, anywhere someone hid. Jesus, she had to stop this swirl of vengeance, the need for retaliation and *justice* on his behalf.

*Easy, Sarah. Breathe.*

He pressed his thumbs into her arch, and she moaned at the release of tension there. As he kneaded her heel and pulled on her toes, she felt her spine relax more than if she'd sat in a hundred baths. She focused her eyes on Steffan, and let her mind process—calmly, objectively—what she'd just learned.

Later, she and Steffan would have words over what she had not known about Laurent. She should have been told by Steffan, if not Laurent, that the man carried trauma from a horrific event that had to have left scars. Was she any better? She hadn't told them about her past, either. It was as if the tragedy won. The irony of her conviction to never forget what had happened to her, yet wanting for *Laurent* to forget, wasn't lost on her. Damn, Steffan and his argument shone a spotlight on her double standard.

Steffan's gaze lazily drifted over her body as he unbuttoned his shirt and tossed it aside. His pants, rumpled from the humidity, hung low on his hips giving her a glimpse of that trail of blond hair that ran down his belly to disappear behind his pants. His appreciation of her nudity tented his pants. That familiar power she felt when admired, when someone willingly offered their services to her, climbed up through her now-relaxing feet to the crown of her head. While Laurent overtly took care of her needs, an odd thought arose how a Dominant could do the same. Steffan appreciated her dominance and understood it from a different vantage point. It was like a peer praising you for being a worthy opponent. Yet, she oddly didn't feel in competition with Steffan.

"Do you believe in fate?" Laurent asked, overturning the thoughts she'd been trying to piece together about this entire, evolving situation.

She shifted her attention to Laurent who'd moved on to her other foot. "No."

"That's okay. I'll believe for the both of us." His charming smile could undo the toughest cynic. "I think I'm here to help you for a reason, if you'll let me."

His fingers moved up her calves, pressing into her muscle to stop at that tender spot behind her knees. He raked his fingers once more down to her ankles. She hadn't taken note of how large his hands were, his palms spanning over her leg as if they were matchsticks.

"I know what it's like to have to overcome something," he said. "After Steffan dragged me home from Amsterdam, I hid out for a while, but then I started talking with Steffan. We played. Steffan insisted I use my voice. Speak out when a line was being crossed. It helped me to know someone was listening to me."

She could see that. He'd had his freedom taken where words probably didn't matter. To then have them matter, it could heal your sense of control. All submissives needed to know there were limits and they'd be honored. She needed a library of rules to feel safe.

"I think perhaps we both need to overcome what happened to us."

"What else happened to you?" Her question came out as a breath as his fingers dug into her calf muscles.

"Dark. They put me in absolute dark. Then I became nothing."

"The blindfolds. It's why they bother you."

"They don't as much anymore, thanks to Steffan."

She glanced up at Steffan. His eyes remained locked on hers. His body was taut with sexual tension.

She pulled her leg free. "Laurent, undress for me. Then make yourself comfortable on the bed."

"Yes, Mistress."

Oh, how she loved those words. *Yes. Mistress.* She rose and stood by the dresser, took in every bit of his movements as he shed his clothes. He folded them carefully, laid them over the stuffed chair in the corner. He then came to her, stopping a foot away. "Where do you want me?"

"Everywhere," she said. "I'm going to give you a gift. You are not nothing. You could never be. I'm going to show you."

In her periphery, she watched Steffan push off the wall. In protest, perhaps? He had said *both of us.*

"Lie down on your back on the bed for me?" she asked.

Laurent did as she asked. She placed one knee on the long, tufted bench at the end of the bed, and picked up an abandoned wrap dress. It was a deep coral, the color of a sea fan she'd seen scuba diving many years ago, and simple, so not to compete with the woman wearing it.

"I'm not going to bind you, Laurent. Do you know why?" She slid the tie through the loops and wrapped the end around one hand.

He shook his head slowly, not an ounce of fear showing in those gorgeous dark eyes.

"I want you to use those talented hands in every way imaginable."

"Thank you, Mistress."

Steffan drifted closer to the bed when she crawled on hands and knees toward Laurent.

"I am, however, going to place this over your eyes." A subtle tension took hold in his jaw as she laid the cloth belt across the beautiful fan of his lashes.

She straddled him, his cock pressing against her pussy, already slick with arousal, and leaned down to whisper in his ear. "Remember your safeword, and know that you're going to get something better than watching me. You're going to feel me. Feel me in the dark."

Steffan's breathing grew more ragged. She peered over her shoulder. He'd divested himself of his pants and shoes, and stood by the bed, his cock in his fist. The man's lack of inhibitions would never cease to amaze her, and she felt her muscles clench a little, now that she'd had him inside her and knew what that cock could do. What she didn't know, however, was Laurent's talents.

She returned her attention to the man beneath her. She loved seeing a man on his back—all that hard muscle laying prostrate, waiting for her. It showed such strength for them to submit this way.

She threaded her fingers through his thick dark curls. "I love your hair. The way it moves in the wind. The way it feels in my hands." His cock twitched under her.

She ran her fingers tips lightly over the tie over his eyes. "Too bad this is a polyester blend."

He smiled. "Won't say it," he said, referencing his safeword.

"You will if you need to, won't you, my sweet man, because I will be very displeased with you if you don't."

"Yes, Mistress."

"Hands above you. Palms on the headboard."

The bed dipped to her left. Steffan's scent, his presence, grew closer.

She eased up between Laurent's elbows, her legs straddling his torso. Her body responded to all that male muscle between her legs, her pussy weeping in seconds. The brush of his soft hair across her belly, those ridges in his abdomen, inflamed her growing lust for this man, something she'd kept in check for far too long. Her breasts brushed across his mouth as she rose up higher on him, slicking his belly with her juice. His tongue darted out, stealing a taste. She tsked.

"Mmm, did I tell you to use that tongue?"

She slid down, bumping against his rigid cock. His hips arched up, seeking and searching for entry.

"Still, my sweet man. Let me ride you."

His chest rose and fell in short pants. "Mistress, whatever you wish."

"I wish for so many things." That truth tumbled out of her lips, emotion creeping in. What was it about this man that so easily forced truth from people? She wished for Laurent to have never gone through what he had. She wished she'd never scened with Troy Myers. She couldn't wish she'd never met Joshua. Perhaps a nice memory of him was her penance for what had occurred.

"Granted," he whispered.

Her eyes pricked. "So, then I will grant something to you." She took his mouth, his tongue instantly moving into action, seeking, searching for hers. She needed to connect with him first this way, the tender touching of lips, the secret message that all kisses provided. For long minutes, she kissed him with all the passion she'd kept contained, all the fury at what he'd been through, and all the love she knew she'd never be able to withhold from him ever again. They were two damaged souls who had found a way to live despite their past. Did that not alone deserve this reward?

She eased herself down so her folds parted on either side of Laurent's erection. Steffan eased himself alongside them, and his hand came down on her back as if he needed the contact. She glanced at him. His eyes held hunger, awe, and yes, love. He honestly didn't mind her riding another man's torso, about to take another man's cock.

"I thought you didn't watch," she said to Steffan.

"Oh, I am participating fully in my mind. Keep going."

She slicked up Laurent's thick length with her wet, and small moans left his throat with each drag and slide. Steffan's hands moved up her spine to her neck, threading fingers through her hair. He massaged the base of her skull so deliciously, and she let herself get lost in the sensation of touching and being touched by both of them. A rush of more fluid came at the thought of how she wanted them—both of them, despite Steffan's harsh arrogance, despite Laurent's goodness that shamed her.

Her own breath puffed from her lips as she glided up and down for long minutes until Steffan's fingers curled against her back and Laurent's breathing was labored from holding himself back.

"What would you give to be inside me?" She stared at Steffan though the question was for Laurent.

"Anything." Laurent's fingers curled into fists as if he was trying to punch through the thick padded fabric of the headboard.

She cupped Laurent's face. "Then, I want you to do something for me. Whenever you're in the dark, remember this feeling." She raised up on her knees positioned his cock at her opening and sank down. Steffan's hands pushed against her lower back as if helping her sink onto him. God, she loved the dual feel of his palm on her and the stretch inside from Laurent's cock.

"Oh, God," Laurent huffed out. His lips quirked up in lust and relief.

Steffan's hands fisted her hair, and he yanked her face to him, mashing his lips to hers. She should have fought it—this taking of her mouth, but the taste of his tongue, the talented way he curved his lips over hers, obliterated any need to break away. She had a man underneath her, straining to stay still for her. That would be enough.

"Mistress." Laurent's voice was strangled, taut with strain from holding himself back.

She broke away from Steffan and brought her lips down to Laurent's.

"Come for me. Don't hold back, and remember what I said about the dark." She rose up and ground herself against him, her clit throbbing in pleasure but not yet cresting over.

He released quickly, arching his back against her. She didn't let pleasure overtake her, not yet.

She dragged the tie from over Laurent's eyes, and he blinked up at her. "Thank you," he mouthed, still panting from his climax. She lay down on his chest, rising and falling with his breaths until they steadied. Only when he freely slipped out of her, did she ease off him. The bed jostled as the three of them moved all at once. Before she could swing her legs over the side, an arm grasped her around her waist.

"You denied yourself." She looked down at the blond hair dusting that forearm. Steffan had moved quickly, lurching over Laurent who pulled himself up to sitting against the headboard.

"Offering?" she asked.

"Yes."

She twisted to face Steffan, his cock hard and ready for her. She *had* denied herself for reasons she couldn't explain. She let herself be pulled into his lap, her legs straddling his. "Laurent's not through with his massage, isn't that right, Laurent?"

Without needing any more direction, Laurent moved in behind her. His hands fell to her shoulders.

"Thank your Mistress for her gift to you, Laurent. Use all that physical therapy education to remove that worry from her shoulders," Steffan said.

Laurent's hands kneaded the tight hard muscles of her upper traps and words of protest died in her throat.

"I'll take care of her lower half." Steffan took her hands and placed them over his cock. "Perhaps you have use for this … Mistress." His mouth quirked up into a sly smile.

"Perhaps."

Steffan's definition of 'perhaps' was broad, because he pulled her higher onto him until his cock nestled against her clit.

"You should have told me." She didn't know why she had to say those words again. Perhaps because she needed him to hear her, really *understand*, what a breach of trust it was to not know the depth of Laurent's pain, even though she'd been no better.

"Yes. Forgive us." Steffan cupped the side of her face. "You should have been told many things, Sarah. Like how you are a gift to people—to me, to Laurent, to so many."

No words would banish her demons, but for a few minutes, they might hold them at bay. She rose up on her knees and sank down on him, his cock stretching her as much as Laurent's, but longer, reaching her furthest point easily. That thudding pain as he neared her cervix didn't stop her from wanting him, wanting to come, so all those words that had crossed her lips and theirs in the last few hours would be erased—if just for a minute. He arched his hips and thoughts were no longer necessary.

Gripping his shoulders, she rode him, hard. Steffan's fingers dug into her hips until bruises formed. Laurent pressed his fingers and knuckles into her muscles, never stopping his massage, as she moved up and down. So many hands were on her, pleasuring her, giving to her.

Male musk rose in her nose, mixed with the Ginger Thomas and jasmine flowers of the night air. In the far-off distance, joining with her low moans of pleasure, the ocean roared while she took her fill of both of them. Her orgasm built and rose like the waves crashing outside. First rising up and then falling into a ripple that radiated down her legs and up her spine. Steffan's mouth was on hers again, swallowing her needy little cries as she ground herself into his pelvis, her breasts pressed into his chest.

Later, when they were lying in the bed together, her body tucked against Steffan's, Laurent curled on his side, his front to her back, sadness replaced her anger. Now that she knew his story, all the pain she felt for Laurent and all the pain she felt for herself mixed together and thumped against her heart. It wasn't going to let go of her, was it? *Not ever.* But she could take care of Laurent. He'd be additional penance. As for Steffan? She couldn't think. Instead, she let the dark take her over.

# 33

Steffan drummed his fingers on the restaurant table and watched as Jonathan strode over with a stormy expression. Steffan nodded to the man as he yanked the chair back, its legs protesting in a scrape along the ridiculous, over-the-top marble floor.

"Thank you for meeting me," Steffan said.

"What's this about?" Jonathan tossed his cell phone in the middle of the small table. He pointed to the text Steffan had sent. *Joshua Martin. Troy Myers. Coffee Bar. 9 a.m.* "Where did you hear those names?"

So Jonathan knew who those men were. Steffan had taken an awfully big chance last night, and he still wasn't sure how it was going to pan out. Sure, they'd had sex, but he woke up this morning to the calm, aloof woman who'd met him in The Library four weeks ago. Gone was the carefree woman who rode waves to the shore. In other words, she was back to her old self, and he knew, deep down, guilt had a stronger hold on her than he could have imagined. He needed more information.

"From Sarah. Last night. Coffee please?" he mouthed a waitress who glanced over at them.

"Fuck." Jonathan grabbed a packet of sugar and waved it to settle the crystals. "That why Sarah hasn't answered her phone or my text. How did this come about?"

"Something I said triggered her."

His waving hand stopped, and Steffan raised his. "It was nothing significant, but apparently it set her off. I found her on the beach, and she told me the story."

He leaned back in his chair as the waitress poured them each a cup of coffee. "What may I get you gentleman, or will you be having the buffet?"

Without looking up at her, he said, "We'll have the buffet, Karen. Thank you."

"How did this happen, Jonathan? And don't tell me it's none of my business. I love her."

Jonathan eyed him. "Well, if she told you about Martin and Myers, believe it or not, she probably loves you back. She's warning you away."

"I get that. Psych 101. Tell me how to reach her." He tried one way last night, which worked for a time.

"Give her space," Jonathan said.

"Not an option."

"Well, sorry there, Steffan, my man, that's what you're going to need to do."

"Bullshit."

"Listen—"

'No, she's been left alone enough, Jonathan, *my man*." He scrubbed his chin. "Shit. Sorry."

Jonathan chuffed. "You do love her."

He hadn't believed him? "Hell, yes."

"Okay, then." Jonathan took in a deep breath. "Joshua Martin was an immature kid. He had everything. Sarah was the first thing in his life he wanted but couldn't have—some-

ELIZABETH SAFLEUR

thing daddy couldn't buy. It was very hard on Sarah as she didn't want to break all ties. She considered his mother, Clementina, the mother she wished she had. When the suicide took place, Sarah ran home hysterical. Clementina followed her and pounded on the front door. Screaming. Crying. Accusing Sarah of killing her son. Claire and my father packed Sarah up and put her on a plane to New York with instructions not to come back any time soon."

"You were there?"

"No. I was a clueless teenager and off at some boy's camp when the shit hit the fan."

"But she told you this story?"

"It took me months to piece together the whole thing, but about a year later, I did get the complete story."

He blew out a long breath. "Good, no one should carry this around alone."

"Good response." Jonathan took a large gulp of coffee. "With our family's reputation in danger, Claire didn't handle it well."

"Shocker."

"I see you've met her."

"No, Laurent did. Didn't take a shine to her, and I trust his judgment implicitly."

"Intuitive man."

"Sarah didn't have therapy or anything? Even after Troy Myers?"

Jonathan cursed. "That was a cluster. But, no, not until she met Alexander. He has his own brand of therapy."

"Protocol." *Rules are what make us who we are.* Those remembered words of hers dropped like lead into his gut. She'd explained the "why" behind all those guidelines she was so fond of. It was her own personal road map of relationships. So long as everyone stuck to the plan, all would be well. He leaned back, aware of the stiffness in his spine. His coffee remained untouched, and he had no appetite for anything.

"It helped," Jonathan said. "Gave her boundaries she felt she lacked. Boundaries that might have had things turn out differently."

"You know that's bullshit, right?"

"I'll give you a pass on that tone because I believe you when you say you love her. But everyone deals with things in their own way. She's had a good life."

"Half a life."

Jonathan apprised him. "And you want to be the other half. So where does that leave Laurent?"

"With us. We've always lived an unconventional life. So why not?" The question was, how to make her seriously consider a permanent three-way relationship. He felt they'd broken through one of her walls last night, but then this morning ... well, if she was afraid of getting involved with one man, two might be overwhelming.

Jonathan stood. "I promised to bring Christiana tea. She gets cranky without it." He looked down at him. "If you really love Sarah—and God help me, if you're fucking with her you'll have more than me to deal with—you'll do what I say. Give her space but be around. If she hasn't asked you to leave, then she needs you."

It wasn't a good enough answer. He glared at the man, his eyes as fierce as the odd mix of rage and compassion that coursed through his veins at his advice. "Is that what you would do?"

"Fuck no. You're talking to the man who gave up his seat in Congress to marry a woman too young, too impression-able, and too innocent for him." He laughed. "Just be there for her. And this may be the worst timing in the world, but you should know, Christiana and I are going to get married here. We're going to have a small ceremony on the beach tomorrow. Sunset. Just the inner circle, Tribunal Council members and significant others. So if you're serious about Sarah, that includes you."

"No Claire?" Steffan asked.

"She may never get over being left out, but I'm fine with it."

Now that Steffan knew more about Sarah's mother, he knew she would be livid—and he was fine with it, too.

She let Sarah live with a terror buried so deep, she'd lost touch with it. Trouble was, he had to figure out how to exorcize a ghost, and he hadn't a clue how to start.

## 34

A sudden burst of warm tropical air puffed out Sarah's dress and the diaphanous fabric teased her calves while the salty, humidity of the Caribbean caressed her skin. She took a sip of champagne. The bubbles tickled the roof of her mouth before cascading over that annoying, persistent lump in her throat. Hundreds of people wished to be where she now sat —on a balcony at a resort in St. Thomas overlooking the gray-blue ocean. Joy should be coursing through her veins. She was lucky. No, she was blessed. *Remember that, Sarah Marie Marillioux.* Plus, she'd confessed her greatest sin. Steffan refused to buy it as a sin, and Laurent, well ... what could she say about that bewitching man?

She'd made some calls this morning and discovered that the Tribunal council in Amsterdam knew all about the Masters of X, and Steffan had been right about their incarceration. It was too good enough for them.

Through a break in the palm trees that led to the beach, she could see Steffan and Laurent roughhousing in the waves. They jumped and threw each other down like teenagers, skin shining in the sunlight. They were a gift to her, one she would enjoy for as long as she could, which meant two more days. Jonathan had announced elopement plans, so all members of the Tribunal Council and their significant others extended their stay with little complaint to see Jonathan and Christiana marry. She chuckled into her glass recalling his text.

<<I'm taking your advice. We're eloping. Tuesday night. Regal's beach. 6 p.m. Don't tell Claire. And don't you dare wear high heels. They'll sink.>>

Her mother was going to have a coronary as all her plans crumbled. Her commands for men's morning suits would be for naught, and the whole of DC society no longer needed to fit themselves into the National Cathedral in two months to watch her stepson, the former U.S. Congressman from Rhode Island, marry the lovely Christiana Snow before Church and God. Ah, well. Best laid plans and all that.

Her plans to hop on the first flight back to DC that morning were dashed as well. Now? She wouldn't be the petulant child who has a tantrum and runs off.

She'd texted Madeline, saying she was taking a few more days off and to reschedule all her appointments to next week. Madeline didn't seem at all surprised. Sarah had done it frequently lately. Her life really was dissolving into a mess of chaotic disorder.

From her balcony perch she caught sight of Alexander striding around the pool, saying hello to the guests who'd stayed behind—Carson, Mark, Ryan, each having their woman nestled alongside them in their bikinis—well, the bottoms anyway. She owed Alexander an apology for her mad dash out of the ballroom the other night. She just didn't know what to say. *Sorry for my drama? Sorry for being wholly inappropriate at such an auspicious occasion?* He hadn't reached out to her either, for which she was grateful.

Steffan's long, lean body stretched out before a wave.

Earlier today, she'd ordered Laurent to lure Steffan out to the beach for a swim. They were beautiful, annoyingly attentive, hovering men who continued to watch her with worried eyes whenever she so much as sniffed. She'd needed some alone time with Christiana. She was going to give her and Jonathan the elopement of their dreams. After all, that's what she was good at—spinning dreams in yards of silk and tulle and sky-high heels, or in Christiana's case, glitter tennis shoes.

A soft knock sounded, signaling Christiana had arrived.

The young girl had said she wanted something that resembled a beach party, not an ounce of formality. Sarah hadn't done a beach wedding in years, so she had to get creative. Madeline was able to pull the dress she'd wanted for Christiana and rush it to Regal, along with linen suits for the men which would always look rumpled but, again, beach. Sarah pulled a number of deep blue silk-blend Hawaiian shirts from one of the Regal shops to pair with the white linen pants. The men would be a picture postcard of tropical casual and chic.

She swung open the door to find Christiana, a blush of sunburn over her nose, holding a garment bag.

"Come in, beautiful bride." Sarah stepped back, but Christiana launched herself at her, engulfing her a bear hug. The plastic garment bag rustled around them.

"You're going to be my sister in a few hours!"

Sarah laughed. No one ever pushed Christiana away. She was like a little secret weapon, the kitten in their group that made eighteen-wheelers stop in the middle of the highway so the little fluff ball could cross the road.

"I am, and your dress arrived," Sarah said. "Nothing like the nick of time."

"Well, about that. I have an idea. Hear me out." She raised the garment bag in her hand. "This is what I wore when

Jonathan first took me to Covil Sereia and we ..." She blushed a deep pink. If Sarah had any question how this woman had toppled her step-brother from bachelorhood to committed man, that doubt faded seeing her innocent reaction to a mere memory. The girl was just so honest. Had Sarah ever been that innocent?

"Well ..." Christiana laid it over a chair and unzipped the bag. She pulled out a cheap, white cotton, sundress. It was so perfectly Christiana. "I want to wear it. I'd have thrown it out years ago, but Jonathan insisted I keep it. Now I want to surprise him. Also, if we could weave in some yellow and blue tropical flowers into my wedding veil, we'll have ... Sarah, are you okay?"

Sarah swiped a finger under her lashes to remove any traces of the emotion leaking from her eyes. "I'm more than fine. Your enthusiasm is catching, and it's a beautiful idea." Christiana's gesture was a stunning display of love, loyalty, and truth. She took the dress and shook it out. "Let's see what we can do. Would you mind if I added a little gold thread along here?" She ran her finger over the neckline. 'Nothing too ... blingy, I believe was your word."

"Anything you do will be fine. I trust you completely."

And with those words, Sarah was in serious danger of losing her composure. She wouldn't allow it as Christiana would worry and now was *not* the time for a bride to worry about a thing.

"Now, what about your father? Was Alexander able to find him in Africa?" she asked.

"Yes. Alexander is amazing. He can make anything happen—like you."

She laughed at that. "Not everything. I didn't stop my mother from the horrid magenta."

"You would have if I'd pressed the issue. You're the most powerful woman I've ever met."

She swallowed back that ever-present lump in her throat and straightened Christiana's tee-shirt, which was always lopsided.

"There you go again," she said with a smile. "I love you, Sarah."

This time she didn't try to stop the tears. Sarah hugged the girl, trying to share all the love she felt for her, and absorb some of her magical, youthful optimism.

"Love you back, Christiana girl." She wasn't like her soon-to-be-sister-in-law. She'd never believed the world was good. She thought you had to *be* good and then good would come. She pulled back, and Christiana swiped at her cheek.

"Look at us? Two emotional women," Christiana said. "It's really happening, isn't it Sarah? Over three years and I'm finally marrying Jonathan. Despite everything."

"Despite everything," Sarah mirrored.

At least something was moving forward.

The door swung open, and Laurent and Steffan tumbled inside, Steffan grinning, having Laurent in a headlock, salt water dripping off his hair—so much like two best friends, a best friend to best friend. He released him once they saw Christiana standing there.

"What did we miss?" Laurent asked.

"Nothing," Sarah said.

"Well, the last of the holdouts are gone," Steffan said. "We saw Seraphina and Michael load into a taxi. Now it's just us and the Tribunal."

"Sounds good to me," Laurent said and tossed a frisbee in the air. "I like our tribe."

Christiana giggled. "Good way to put it, Laurent. Tribe Tribunal."

*Belonging.* It was a human need to be part of a tribe, to belong to something greater than yourself. It's what Accendos, and inside that, the Tribunal Council, had been for her for so long. Now her tribe had changed. Derek already had children, and she didn't seem him often. How soon before Carson and London moved further south, something they both had talked about? Or, Jonathan and Christiana? Christiana said children weren't in the cards but that could change overnight, and Sarah would ensure they'd be the best-dressed children in DC. She supposed change was the price for living—and she, too, would put some changes in place when she got home, starting with moving into Accendos full-time.

"Laurent, why don't you pour us some more champagne?" she asked. "The next two days are going to be about celebrating Christiana and Jonathan." She raised her glass. She could do this. She could be whoever they needed.

## 35

The soft steel drum tinkled through the air. Not exactly Pachelbel's canon, but the music was light and festive, which is what Christiana had asked for. Once the girl understood her wishes would be honored, she'd turned into a power-house of requests. Music was just the beginning. *Fairy lights—hundreds, no, thousands of them. And, flowers and tiki torches, and leis for everyone and umbrella drinks.* "Not a single champagne flute within a hundred miles," she'd said. Sarah drew the line at coconut shell glasses. They'd compromised on brightly colored plastic wine goblets. "With umbrellas," Christiana had countered. Never again would she consider Christiana weak, but then she'd never thought the girl was—or any submissive for that matter. Laurent also proved that theory —repeatedly.

He brought her espresso in the morning and a second cup precisely at 4 p.m. when she liked that second hit of caffeine. He rubbed her feet when she was on the hundred calls a "simple beach wedding" demanded, threatening her ability to form sentences with his wickedly strong fingers. Then, there was the magic of his tongue. She wasn't sure she'd ever take another shower again without thinking of how he could bring her to orgasm in under two minutes from his knees, his hands boxed behind his back.

She let Steffan watch, his confident, cool blue eyes never once showing he was upset being relegated to voyeur. Perhaps to allow her to display her control? The fact he never once questioned her only grew her irritation. The man was just so … unwavering in his calm. She now understood more deeply how a submissive might brat to get a rise out of someone. The only saving grace was his lusty appetite for her body never diminished. She'd find herself atop him in the middle of the night, his cock rigid as steel and finding her greedy pussy with little need for guidance, as if he'd ever take direction anyway.

Sarah stepped down the four stone steps leading to the circular terrace where the ceremony would be held. Steffan and Laurent had escorted her down the elevator, but she'd asked Laurent to fetch some last-minute items, including the flower petals and birdseed, people would throw in the air—another Christiana request—after the vows. Steffan joined the men, quickly, heartily accepting a flask from Derek.

"I thought I said no heels."

She turned to find Jonathan's green eyes twinkling down at her in the twilight.

"Did you think I'd obey?" she asked with raised eyebrows.

"Not on your life." He pecked her on the cheek.

"You look wonderful, Jay. Happiness suits you," she said. "You're finally getting what you want."

"Yes. Legal marriage. Who knew?"

"I still can't believe you sent in a marriage application months ago to St. Thomas. Had this planned all along?"

"I like to be prepared for any inevitability. I had once

thought I had her almost convinced on a destination wedding. Then Claire stepped in …"

She raised her hand. "Please, no mother talk today. I'll think about breaking the news to her later."

He ran a finger over his lip. "Thank you, Sarah."

"You know you don't have to thank me."

"No, I do. Thank you for sticking by me, always."

Her throat clogged with love for her stepbrother, who'd been more family to her than any of her full-blooded relatives. "We stick together, Jay." Their childhood—all the ups and downs, the secrets and lies, the pressures of being raised in the public spotlight—wasn't something they discussed often, but the understanding that streamed between them didn't require words.

"Now today," she said, placing her hand on his heart. "Is for the future."

He took in a deep breath. "It is." He snagged two purple plastic goblets from a tray from a server who appeared by his side. He handed her one. "To us. To finding love."

She wasn't going to argue with him. He'd seen her out and about with Steffan and Laurent—their mere presence at this intimate gathering told her exactly what the others thought of them. They'd accepted them into their fold, and unless Sarah cast them out, they'd be welcomed at the most intimate moments of their lives.

"Go," she said. "Enjoy the last few minutes of your life as a bachelor."

He grinned at her and rejoined the men. Derek handed him the flask, which he heartily upended. She laughed a little at watching Carson pluck the little umbrella from his drink and drop it into London's glass, therefore maintaining his male dignity.

"Animals," she said under her breath. God, she loved those men. They could not be tamed, but then neither could she.

ELIZABETH SAFLEUR

She sipped the cool white wine from her goblet, ignoring the telltale plastic smell, and made a quick pass around the circular terrace. She was pleased to see Derek had managed to commandeer every string of fairy lights on the island. Hundreds of strands were draped under the angled stretch of white canvas, shielding the small crowd underneath.

The casual atmosphere didn't stop the women from dressing to the nines. London, tucked into Carson's side, wore a long blue column dress that set off the collar encircling her throat. The wingtips of a Phoenix bird with rubies for eyes stretched across her collarbone, a symbol of how her Master viewed her—strong and unsinkable, and he'd be sure she'd stay that way. Isabella touched her thick metal collar, a striking contrast against her ruched flesh-colored dress that hugged her curves, almost as close as her Master. Marcos kept a close hold on her. Samantha's ears dripped with a waterfall of diamonds which Sarah knew wouldn't last long by the way her little girl's fists kept clutching at the sparkly things. Derek took the little squirming bundle in his arms and tossed her in the air, a delighted giggle enthralling everyone within earshot.

Her gaze drifted to the beach. Alexander stood alone facing the waves, hands in his pockets, his white linen suit rumpled and ruffling in the breeze. He could pose for a tourism ad. His eyes were fixed on the red and gold clouds signaling Jonathan and Christiana would have a beautiful sunset for their ceremony. His brow furrowed as if he was deep in thought. As soon as she wondered about what, he turned and caught her gaping at him. He smiled, and he strode over.

"I'm sorry, Alexander. I didn't mean to spy on you." A rush of emotion floated on her whisper.

"Sarah, you don't ever apologize to me." He put his arm

226

around her and pulled her in. "You and I are beyond such things. No matter whose blood courses through our veins, I consider you my daughter. You remember that." He looked down at her. "And remember who you are."

His words were not meant to be an admonishment, but somehow she felt they should be.

"I've been thinking," she said. "About moving to Accendos permanently."

"It's your home, Sarah. You are always welcomed, but are you sure?"

"It's for the best."

He picked up her hand—the second time this weekend. "Is it?"

"Do you know, you may be the only man in the world who could carry off a wrinkled suit?" Things had gotten entirely too serious, and today wasn't about her anyway.

He chuckled. "I must say it's comfortable." He dropped her hand. "Let's go and marry those two before Jonathan throws Christiana over his shoulder and marches down to the courthouse for this thing."

"He can't. I spent an hour on those flowers in her hair."

Alexander joined Jonathan at the end of the terrace, the ocean at their backs. The second they took their positions, all eyes turned to the two of them. The steel drums in the corner stopped and picked up a new tune, something she didn't recognize but which had a soft, melodic rhythm. Jonathan's lips parted, and she followed where his eyes led. Christiana stood at the top of the stairs, her arm hooked through her father's. The man beamed, his usual cargo pants and polo shirt replaced with a smashing outfit of khaki shorts and a white Hawaiian shirt. A shower of blue Alla-manda, yellow hibiscus and Ginger Thomas flowers were woven into Christiana's hair and cascaded down her wedding veil that floated on the ocean breeze. Her dress had been pressed to perfection, and Sarah had one of the on-site tailors embroider gold threads along the neckline and straps so the sparkle would frame her décolletage.

Sarah let her gaze drift back to Jonathan, watched him widen his stance, his arms falling to his side. His attention was so fixed on Christiana, she believed if she was closer to him she might see a reflection of her in his eyes. He was riveted.

Christiana and her father stepped down, the crowd's faces following their procession up the terrace. When she was a few feet away, Jonathan couldn't stop himself and stepped forward to meet her. Peter didn't let go of her arm at first, his eyes holding a slight challenge. Jonathan nodded once at him, and Peter relented. He drew Christiana's hand from his arm. "I love you, Chrissy," he said in a hoarse whisper.

"And, I love you, Dad." She pecked him on the cheek.

As with many father-daughter relationships, they'd had a complicated relationship, but one that had grown better over the last few years. Sarah was glad Alexander had moved mountains to ensure Peter could be here. Then again, that's what Alexander did—took care of others. He was who she should mirror herself after. Someone who did the right thing —always.

Jonathan and Christiana faced one another.

"You wore it."

"Yes." She ran her hand down the front of her sundress.

The flap of the canvas overhead and the clang of lights against tent poles filled the space—and love, so much love, that the tight vise in her heart, the one she'd been living with for the last two days, squeezed once more. Tears leaked from her eyes. A male body pressed into her back, and Steffan's hand settled on her hip, his favorite place to hold her. Laurent was next to her, his hand reaching for her fingers.

She allowed both, as now was not a time to eschew any tender gesture.

"Friends and family, we are gathered here today to witness the joining of Jonathan Franklin Brond and Christiana Snow in marriage," Alexander began.

She laced her fingers through Laurent's. She wanted to feel his presence, this man who was so eager to please her. She then let herself grow lost in Alexander's words.

The ceremony was brief with Jonathan and Christiana reciting vows they had written. Christiana spoke of belonging. "We needed to find each before we could have a life—our real life," she had said, earning a hushed *amen* from Laurent. Jonathan wiped tears from under Christiana's eyes and promised for as long he lived, they were the last tears she'd ever shed unless they were from happiness.

At one point, Christiana placed her hand on his pec and looked up at him with such love and admiration, Sarah's throat threatened to close with the purity of it all, and it was the first time she'd ever seen Jonathan almost break. He quickly swallowed back whatever had risen up. He firmed his jaw, and his resolve returned. If there was one thing she knew about her step-brother—the only other person she was as close to as she was to Alexander—he would do anything for the woman standing in front of him which, to him, meant never breaking. My, how familiar that felt. It was safer that way, was it not? To never be a burden to anyone.

"Jonathan, do you take Christiana to be yours?" Alexander's voice rang out.

"I do."

"And Christiana, do you take Jonathan to be yours?"

"I do, I do, I do."

Jonathan's face cracked into a huge smile at her enthusiasm. A few tittering sounds of approval sounded all around.

"Good. I now pronounce you husband and wife. You may kiss the—"

Christiana leapt up to Jonathan, wrapped her legs around his waist and pressed her lips on his, earning cheers from Marcos and Carson. Isabella clapped, and Derek's little girl screamed in glee at the adults' sudden enthusiasm.

When Christiana broke the kiss, she smiled at her now-husband. "You're mine now."

The smooth back of the dress was now wrinkled and puckered, and the flowers in her hair were mashed into the veil and her back.

"And you will always be mine." Jonathan's fingers dug into her ass, and her lips parted with the silent message. She may have leapt into his arms, but he was the one keeping her there.

Steffan pressed into Sarah's body more, and she realized she'd been leaning into him throughout the ceremony.

As they left the terrace to go inside to the small room for the intimate reception, bird seed and petals rained down on them. She clapped a hand to her mouth. She'd forgotten to distribute them. How did this happen?

"I figured you'd want me to hand them out," Laurent said.

"Good man," she said.

The reception was in the intimate, upscale restaurant on the roof, the sunset spreading out in all directions. Shells, large glass balls from fishermen's nets, and small ice sculptures of mermaids and fish adorned a large oval table. No one sat right away, rather mixing and mingling around the bar, taking in the view.

Jonathan clinked his glass with a fork. "I have one more announcement before we sit down."

Mark and Carson groaned good-naturedly.

"You'll survive another ten minutes," Jonathan chided with a smile.

"Given how long it took you to get her to the altar, that's nothing," Mark called out.

*Animals.*

Jonathan brought out a long black box from behind the bar. "A wedding gift." He handed it to Christiana.

"Jonathan." She took it. "Now I'm going to have to do that *thing* to you tonight."

Wolf calls sounded from the men, their woman shifting on their feet, giving them good-natured sideways glances.

She cracked open the case, her lips parting on a sigh. She drew out a choker, lined with diamonds, sapphires, and pearls, a mother of pearl mermaid dangling between two shells dusted in diamond dust. She peered up at him, her eye alight.

"My little mermaid," he said. "Luring me to—"

"Don't say death," she whispered.

"No, to my life. It's what we do for each other. We bring each other to life." He kissed her on the forehead.

She turned and lifted her hair, and as Jonathan fastened the choker around her neck, the other Dominants in the room visibly straightened. Ryan stood from his stool and pulled Yvette closer in between his legs. Carson widened his stance behind London. Mark placed his hand around the back of Isabella's neck. They did that, absorbed the energy in the room. It wasn't a formal collaring ceremony like Charlotte's, but Jonathan's gesture was intimate and equally profound.

Sarah glanced around at the others in the room, each of them meeting her eyes, some acknowledging with a dip of a head or a smile. That's what her group did. They belonged to each other so completely, they didn't need words.

She exchanged a glance with Jonathan. His eyes softened toward her before returning his attention to the love of his life. That's when she put a name to that chronic hollow feeling inside her—despite all the people in the room who would protect her, love her, she was estranged—and it was of her own making. She had two men who were offering themselves to her, and she'd done what? Thrown it back in their faces.

She looked at Laurent, chatting up Yvette a few feet away. He glanced her way as if sensing her staring at him. He winked at her, the playful little sub. He then arched his eyebrows in question. She knew what he was asking. *What do you need?* Steffan, standing at the bar, also glanced at her. It was as if the three of them were held together by an invisible thread, knowing when one pulled away or went in a different direction. They were bound to one another—inexplicably connected.

They continued to stare at her, softly, and it was killing her. This time she wouldn't be strong enough to resist them. She'd break rules. She'd not be able to stop herself. She needed both of them. Not wanted. *Needed.*

She turned to Derek. "I understand you, Samantha, and the kids are flying back tonight."

His brow furrowed. "Yes. Wheels up at 10 p.m." He glanced at Steffan who studied her as if he was attempting to read her thoughts.

"Lots of planes leaving from here this week, however," Derek said.

He knew. They all knew, didn't they? For the first time in two decades, she hadn't a clue what to do next. She should go to her room and pack, leave with them, start anew. She could arrow through the small crowd and fall into Steffan and Laurent's arms. She glanced out the glass windows. Or, she could run down to the ocean and throw herself into the waves, take in the cold until she woke up from whatever dream had been cast around her.

She kissed a startled Derek on the cheek. "Love to Samantha and the kids."

The beach would be empty, and the stars and moonlight across the water had looked so magical. She needed the ocean, where the souls of mermaids and lost sailors might have answers.

## 36

Steffan tried to catch Sarah's attention before the elevator doors closed, but she looked so deep in thought it was as if she wasn't seeing anything or anyone.

A male hand came down on his shoulder. "Sarah asked if we were flying back tonight." Derek cocked an eyebrow at him. "Is she?"

"Hell no."

"Just what I thought."

Steffan slammed his empty tumbler down on a tray. "Excuse me, Derek." Like hell she was running. Sex notwithstanding, he'd given her two days of space. Enough was enough. He wove through people, each step as if he slogged through molasses.

As soon as he stepped off the elevator, he caught her pushing her way through a glass door down the hallway. She was headed to the beach. If she tried to do anything foolish … He broke into a jog.

She was unwrapping her dress. Fabric floated through the air, and she ran straight into the waves, her hips slapping against a crest tipped in silver moonlight. She arched like a dolphin, cutting through the surface, then disappeared, her head breaking through a few feet away. Shit, it was dark, and she was in the water.

He kicked off his shoes, ripped his shirt straight down, the buttons easily giving away, and peeled it off as he ran to the shoreline. His feet hit the cold water, and he leapt into the waves, diving into the smooth surface. He kicked his legs hard, striving to get to her. When he finally reached Sarah, her dark eyes glinted in the moonlight and the ambient light from the party lights less than one hundred feet away. She didn't look surprised to see him.

She kicked toward him, wrapped her legs around his waist and pressed her breasts against him. Her lips fell onto his, softly at first and then with more hunger. This was not the greeting he'd expected.

When she broke her kiss, he smoothed her hair off her forehead. "I saw Jaws on TV when I was a kid, so I want credit for diving in after you."

She laughed lightly, her teeth flashing white in the dark. "I didn't think anything scared you." She let her head fall back, and he loosened his arms so she could float backward, her hair forming a dark fan waving just under the water surface. A large wave made them bob up and down.

"Everyone's afraid of something," he said. "Like you're afraid of me."

She lifted her head. "I'm not."

He pulled her close again and since he could stand on the sandy bottom, he twirled them around so he could get more light on her face. "Let me re-phrase. You're afraid to love me because you have the power to undo me. Well, let me tell you. You don't. I'm not going to crumble under you, Sarah."

"Said the Dominant male." She gave him a flirty smirk. Her nipples brushed across his pec, and his cock twitched like the animal it was around her.

"I'd expect you to say nothing less," she said. "It's not in our nature to give into our weaknesses."

"Oh, but we all have weak spots. That's not what makes us Dominant, and you know it. What makes us Dominants is our ability to control ourselves. We don't control others—not really. We accept the willing and temporary suspension of power. We can't hurt another without them being willing to accept our control. Just like you couldn't have—"

"Don't." The struggle in her voice nearly broke his heart. "Don't say those names," her whisper barely audible over the sound of the lapping waves.

"It wasn't your fault." He placed his forehead on hers, then captured her lips again, the taste of salt and Sarah. He parted her lips with his tongue, forced her mouth to open more. Her lips barely accepted him. He could feel her hesitation, her withdrawal from anything pleasurable the second she thought of the tragedy of Joshua and the madness of Troy. Anger that her family had let her down, let her blame *herself* for Joshua's despair rose hard, and he pressed his lips harder as if he could stamp out her past.

"Sarah, I love you," he growled into her mouth.

She sucked in a breath and yanked her head back.

"Don't. Admire me. Work with me. Appreciate me, but …"

"But, what? Not love you so deeply that if you were to reject me, I might harm myself? Not happening, sweetheart. I won't leave Laurent, remember? I gave you space the last two days, but that's over." A wave took them up and down again. "You could walk away from me—in those death heels—but it would be a mistake, and you'd regret it. Not now. Not next week. Hell, maybe not next year. But you will someday." He set his forehead against hers. "I know because I made a big one two years ago. I let you get on that plane in London, and I've regretted it ever since."

"You couldn't have stopped me."

"I should have tried." He swirled her again. He could stay for hours like this, his hands on her ass, her crotch pressed against him. "So don't reject me because you have the power to hurt me. Reject me if you don't love me at all."

Splashing made him turn his head to find Laurent appearing next to her. He had followed, as Steffan knew he would. Someone was in need and hurting, so Laurent would be there.

"I'm not rejecting you." She cupped Laurent's face and then turned her gaze back to him. "I have an idea. Something I've been thinking about. I'm going to move into Accendos. We can meet there. It will be—"

"Not good enough. I won't let you disappear into protocol and contracts and what else you're proposing, in sacrifice of something real."

"You can't take that away from me."

He understood what "that" meant—something that could be a barrier between her and others. "I'm not. I'm saying let's have both."

Laurent positioned himself behind her, drew her wet hair over her shoulder.

"How did you learn, Sarah?" Steffan said. "You may have always had controlling characteristics, but how did you learn to execute your dominance?"

"Alexander."

"He took that natural part of you and helped you channel it. What you've never had is an *adult* loving relationship. Let Laurent and I be your teachers there. Alexander gave you one kind of structure, let us show you another."

"Messy," she said. "What I'm proposing is better."

"Yes, it will be messy … and different. What you propose is not good enough. I promise you, your formal dominance and our lives can co-exist."

"Please," Laurent said. "Don't let go of that."

Sarah laughed. "You're impossible." She leaned her head back against his shoulder.

"You deserve more. Like Laurent. He deserves you, don't you think?"

"Trick question. If I say no, it means I don't believe in him. If I say yes, you're forcing me to say I'm worthy of him."

"You are," Laurent placed a kiss on her shoulder. "Mistress."

"And you're my equal," Steffan said.

She tightened her grip on his shoulders. "Except in arrogance."

He laughed.

"There's an old myth," Laurent placed his arms around the two of them and twirled them easily in the water. "That a man and woman were separated by the Gods because they were frightened of how strong they were together. They were then left to search their whole lives for the halves they lost. So I say, let the Gods be afraid because we've beaten them at their game. We're three, and we've found each other."

"That's beautiful." Tears shone in Sarah's eyes. "But you say that now …

"Then we'll believe for you until you're ready to know it."

He could tell Laurent pressed himself into Sarah as her body mashed further into his.

"I could have left two hours ago," she said. "but I didn't. I couldn't. Not without you both."

"So both of us, you will have."

Steffan tightened his hold on her. "There's a suite upstairs with a massive king-sized bed. And we're going to show you how much you can have."

## 37

Sarah grasped Steffan's cock at the root and pulled it through her soaped-up fist until the thick head crossed her palm. He groaned in appreciation and caught her wrist before she could do it again. They hadn't made it to the bed, instead, washing off the salt and sand from their bodies in the open, crescent-shaped shower. It was as if they stood inside a large conch shell.

"I love you, Sarah." His blue eyes glinted in the dark. The only light came from tiny twinkle lights, recessed and inlaid the tile meant to resemble stars.

"And I love you." She glanced down at Laurent on his knees. "Both of you." She'd given up trying to fight what was happening between the three of them. Truth was, she'd run out of *reasons* to fight them.

"Did your mistress say you could touch yourself, Laurent?"

The man had eyes in the back of his head.

His hands dropped to his sides. "No, sir."

"Mistress, Sarah," Steffan said. "What do you wish Laurent to do?"

"Focus."

"Hmmm, vague, but I can roll with it. Laurent, take care of your Mistress." He spun her so her back was to his front. Water pounded on the back of Laurent as he knelt. Steffan's palm slid down her belly to part the folds of her labia with his fingers. His fingers slid easily down only to pinch her swollen clit between his first and second finger. He pulled it forward as if offering.

"Wicked man."

"Wish me to stop?"

"Not on your life."

"Hands boxed behind your back, Laurent."

As soon as his arm were behind him, she grasped handfuls of his hair and pulled his head closer. "Taste me."

His tongue reached out to flick her captured clitoris. Steffan's cock pressed into her back, urging her pelvis forward. Laurent's mouth latched on, and he sucked and licked until her writhing couldn't be contained. Steffan hooked his legs around her ankles, holding her legs open, and his arm banded her to him, his other hand holding her crotch steadily. She could have told him to stop his infernal topping, but Laurent's mouth was driving her mad with desire. He had no trouble following her bucking pelvis. When his whole mouth took her throbbing bud, the demands of her sex grew urgent.

"Fuck me with your mouth," she demanded, and came so hard Steffan had to hold her upright. As she came down, she gulped in the steam that had risen thickly until long lines of water ran down the tiles all around them.

"Now," she said. "You'll let me take your cock. Inside me."

"I would be honored." He stood.

She freed herself from Steffan so Laurent could lift her up, his large hands palming her ass. He turned her so she could see Steffan's eyes fire, his jaw clench, over his shoulder.

She'd grant this gift to Laurent, to be inside her like this
—*occasionally.* It would be good for Steffan to remember she
was as Dominant as he, and perhaps trying to hold her still
like he had—even in the name of pleasure—wasn't wise. It
was something they'd work on.

Laurent proved to be as strong as Steffan in holding her,
pounding into her, and when she finally let him come inside
her, he called out *love you, Mistress*, over and over. She
believed she matched his orgasm from hearing those words
alone.

They finally did make it to the bed. They dozed, but she
awoke often, a mouth on her breast again or she'd climb on
top of Steffan and take his cock inside her. Or she'd wake up
coming, Laurent's mouth on her pussy under the damp
sheets. Steffan's mouth would find hers, swallowing all the
pain she released in her cries as she came, all the natural
human fears that came when something new was being
birthed. They didn't hide their want of her, and she let them
want her.

She awoke just before the light cracked over the horizon
and peeked through the curtains. That claw of guilt she'd
been living with inexplicably let go like a fist unclenching. It
was like a dark cloud had receded and exposed the brilliant
sun, stripping away all the memories until they were
bleached bones. She audibly gasped at the open space left in
its place. A curious sensation of lightness nearly took her
breath away, and she nearly soared to the ceiling. A heavy
arm across her rib cage and another male leg across her thigh
pinned her to the mattress. If she did float off the bed, they
wouldn't let her go alone.

When light fully breached the room, she turned her head
to one man and then to the other and memorized their
profiles. She would fill this new empty space with her love
for these two men, and let them love her. Oh, they'd have a

contract. She needed one. Perhaps, however, she'd wrap it in all the desire and affection she felt for these two, bossy, relentless, overly-optimistic men. She'd see how it felt. Try it on, as Steffan had suggested. For now, she was, as some like to say, *all in.*

# Epilogue

Sarah lifted her face to the sunshine, her palms soaking in the warmth from the stones under her hands.

Sticky summer was going to take hold soon. They'd be forced inside into the air conditioning. But for now, she'd sit on the terrace steps of Alexander's gardens, shoes by her side. Laurent was still moving his clothes into her closet in her room upstairs, and Steffan was home, making the three of them dinner. She, Steffan, and Laurent would have to take a larger room at Accendos soon. For now, she rather liked the closeness, being crammed together, their scents mixing on the clothes.

Her phone buzzed with an incoming text. <<for dinner, homemade pasta or Moroccan stew>>

She texted back. <<salad>>

<<not on your life>>

<<overbearing Dominant>>

<<unimaginative Domme>>

She let a few seconds tick by, and sure enough, another text from Steffan came in. <<veggies in the pasta>>

<<sold>

This compromise thing wasn't so bad.

She texted back. <<hold the pasta>>

She wasn't going to get carried away with optimism, however.

He didn't answer, and she laughed. He wouldn't listen, but that was okay. Laurent would make sure she had a salad on the side, which she'd eat. The two of them were constantly pushing food on her. Who was she to complain? Well, maybe her waistline. She'd gone up an entire dress size since Steffan and Laurent moved into her townhouse, though both of them promised—the liars—sex burned as many calories as Steffan could dish onto a plate.

She heard a male's footstep behind her.

"Sarah, just the woman I was looking for," Alexander said.

"Need me to vet another member? Because I have my hands full with two men already."

It'd become their little joke. Every time a new member wanted to join, Alexander reminded her not to expand her "collection" too quickly. A reverse harem did sound wonderful—one man to cook, one to rub her feet, and now maybe a third to … do what? She had everything she needed, and she'd never cheat on her two men.

"I thought you'd be directing Laurent on the great closet redistribution. Carrie tells me he's finally putting his clothes into your closet upstairs."

"Yes, I told him to rearrange everything."

"That will keep him busy for a while, but then he does love to please you. By the way, have you decided?"

"We're thinking a double ceremony, a collaring for Laurent, wedding for us. I don't need the wedding part, but Steffan insisted *he* did, and I love him, so I said yes." Saying the words aloud felt strange but oddly right. The three of them had drawn up a one-page contract that included expectations, dos and don'ts and other important rules and tacked it up on the kitchen wall. It wasn't formal, but it would do for now.

"You could get married here." His gaze wandered over the gardens.

"Yes, this is where I want it to be. Thank you. I was hoping you would offer."

"I'm glad you found Steffan and Laurent, Sarah. You deserve to be happy."

"We all do." His paternal turn wasn't unexpected given the

conversation. "You know, I never believed that whole soul mate thing."

"No one does until they meet him or her."

"You believe in it?"

"I know it exists. I've …" he let the words die on his lips.

The question she'd always wanted to ask hung like lead on her tongue. She knew a little about Alexander's past, his ability to love both men and women, and how he'd once gambled, loved, and lost. She even knew his name. If she was ever going to ask Alexander more about his past, now was the time.

"Was Charles the one for you?" she asked.

"Perhaps. But as you know, it couldn't last." His eyes held such sadness, she felt a tickle in her sinuses. She wouldn't dare ask him for more. She didn't want to see that hurt in his eyes grow.

"I don't know what to say, Alexander."

"I know." And he was back. Calm, confident, steel gray eyes so sure, gazed down on her. For some reason it made her want to cry—to know he had something in his past that could crack that indefatigable exterior. She understood how crushing memories could be, and if he didn't want to talk about it, she wouldn't press him. Timing was everything.

He stood. "You know. Someday, I'd like this to be yours. Accendos, the Tribunal. If you'd have it."

"But Ryan—"

"Doesn't want it. He wants to be with Yvette, and Yvette has no desire to have another man taken from her due to work."

"But it's okay for me?" she laughed lightly.

"Well, let's say … women are better at juggling." He winked at her.

"I'd be honored, Alexander. But you're not thinking of going somewhere are you?"

"Oh, no. There's time. I have no plans on dying yet. And, I hear 60 is the new 40. Or so Christiana says."

"Without Accendos, whatever would you do with yourself, Alexander?"

"I'm not sure, but something will arise. It always does." He smiled, hesitated a minute, but then strode out, leaving her to the gardens, to her thoughts, and to her future. Head of the Tribunal? She liked the sound of that.

"Master Rockingham." Laurent dipped his head in respect.

"Well, Laurent, did it turn out as well as you'd hoped?"

"Better. I need to thank you for your help."

"So, what's wrong?"

Damn, nothing got by this man. "Nothing."

"Laurent."

"I feel like I should confess. I mean, tell them …"

"It's up to you, but I don't know if they really need to know you and I managed this situation. You're satisfied with how it ended up?"

"More than. It's just if it ever got out that I came to you …"

"It would do what? I've never seen Sarah so happy."

"I've never seen Steffan so happy."

"And, you are?"

"Oh, yes, I wanted both of them. Not sure I deserve both, but—"

"Laurent, never underestimate your worth. It is a disservice to your Master and Mistress."

Jesus, the man's tone made him want to drop to his knees.

"If they ever ask me if you came to me, asked for my help to push the three of you together, I will tell them the truth.

You wanted Sarah and Steffan to have each other. You wanted to be with both of them. Now you are."

"Okay." Laurent could live with that. He looked up at the man who had made all this happen, more than Steffan and Sarah might ever know.

Alexander cocked his head as if studying him. "You remind me of someone I knew a long time ago."

"Someone?"

"Yes, another man who was too good for this world."

"What happened?"

"Oh, that's a story for another day." He looked around. "Nice job on the closet. Color coordinated always works for me, as well."

"Thank you. I don't know what she'd do without me." He laughed.

"Agreed. See you around, Laurent."

He hoped so. He felt a little guilty for taking Sarah away from him. He knew they were close. So he sent a wish to the heavens. *Whatever magic you made happen for us, please send some of it to Alexander.*

~The End~

If you loved FEARLESS, you'll love Alexander's story, INVINCIBLE.

Alexander Rockingham keeps the secrets of Washington's most elite players, but none are as devastating as his own. In his own words, "People say a broken heart can kill, but it's really the secrets that take you down."

*Available now at your favorite online retailer or in print from Amazon. Or request it from your local library or favorite bookstore.*

# ABOUT THE AUTHOR

Elizabeth SaFleur writes romance that dares to "go there" from 28 wildlife-filled acres, dances in her spare time and is a certifiable tea snob.

Find out more about Elizabeth on her web site at www. ElizabethSaFleur or join her private Facebook group, Elizabeth's Playroom.

Follow her on Instagram (@ElizabethLoveStory) and TikTok (@ElizabethSaFleurAuthor), too!

### Also by Elizabeth SaFleur
Elite
Holiday Ties
Untouchable
Perfect
Riptide
Lucky
Fearless
Invincible

The White House Gets A Spanking
Spanking the Senator

Tough Road
Tough Luck

Tough Break
Tough Love

Made in the USA
Monee, IL
17 May 2022

96546465R00152